Roberto's Bat

by Allen B. Boyer

SUMMIT
BOOKS

Perfection Learning®

Cover and inside Illustrations: Dan Hatala

About the Author

Allen Boyer lives just outside of Hershey,
Pennsylvania, with his wife, Suzanne. Growing up, he
loved playing ball with his neighborhood friends. His
father was a pitcher and told him stories about his
baseball exploits in high school, college, and the army.
Mr. Boyer is a graduate of Millersville University and
Penn State.

Dedication

For Ken, who was never afraid to swing; for Andy,
who stood tall and proud on the mound; and for Kent,
who was always ready to play

For information, contact
Perfection Learning® Corporation
1000 North Second Avenue, P.O. Box 500
Logan, Iowa 51546-0500.
Phone: 1-800-831-4190
Fax: 1-800-543-2745
perfectionlearning.com

1 2 3 4 5 6 PP 07 06 05 04 03

Paperback ISBN 0-7891-6149-4
Cover Craft® ISBN 0-7569-1642-9

Table of Contents

1

ONE HIT

The Hart Sharks had lost the first three games of their baseball season and were well on their way to losing their fourth. Trailing the Sandbridge Waves for most of the game, the Sharks were trying to make a comeback. Things started looking up when one of the Sharks got a hit in the bottom of the ninth. The players cheered when yet another teammate got a hit. Suddenly, the Sharks had a chance to win this game. All the Sharks were yelling and clapping about the possibility of a comeback. All the Sharks were happy—except one.

Luke Tyson was the only member of the Hart Sharks not excited by his team's late-game rally. He was the only one who sat quietly while his team, behind by two runs, gained a chance to win the game. Around him, Luke could hear his teammates clapping and yelling words of encouragement. They needed Thad Lockhart, a short, round boy with a neck as thick as his head, to get a hit. Luke watched as Thad swung wildly at the first two pitches thrown at him, missing completely. More than anyone else, Luke held his breath when he saw Thad swing for the third and final time, and not just because Thad was his best friend. Now with two outs and everyone watching, Luke was up.

Luke could feel all of his teammates staring at him. He was still looking for his first hit of the season, and his teammates knew it. Well into their fourth game of the year, Luke could sense that his teammates weren't expecting much from him. The clapping and yelling suddenly went from enthusiastic to halfhearted politeness. As Luke walked out of the dugout, he noticed that none of his teammates held up a hand for a high five. He knew it when he stood in the batting circle, took a few swings, and glanced back at the dugout. Heads were already hung in defeat. Luke quietly turned to the crowd. His parents were talking to each other, not even noticing it was his turn at bat.

"Look over your pitches, Luke," he heard his coach advise.

Luke slowly made his way to the plate. He pulled the bat up on his shoulder, took a deep breath, and then focused on a rather tall pitcher staring down at him from the mound.

"Easy out!" he heard the Waves catcher shout.

Luke watched the first pitch come in. He held his breath and swung. He missed. Turning to his teammates who sat quietly on the bench, he noticed that some of them were shaking their heads. Luke turned back to the pitcher, waited for the next pitch, and swung. This time, he heard the sound of his bat hitting the ball. Luke dropped the bat and ran to first base, only to see the pitcher jog under an easy fly ball and make the catch. Just like that—the game was over. The Hart Sharks had lost. Luke had yet to get his first hit.

As he walked back to the dugout, Luke noticed how the Waves pitcher was greeted by his teammates with slaps on the back and high fives. Luke stood for a moment, watching the Waves pitcher smile and laugh with his teammates. Then Luke saw the pitcher walk over to where his parents were standing. He watched the pitcher's parents greet him with smiles and hugs. They were clearly proud of their son. They were also a happy family.

When Luke saw his parents, they weren't even aware that the game was over. Instead, they were still seated, pointing at each other and involved in a loud discussion. It was something they were doing more lately. Luke wished he could get them to stop. As he dropped his bat into the equipment bag, one thought filled Luke's mind—how with one hit, he could have won the game. How with one hit, his teammates would know he was a good baseball player. How with one hit, his parents would be smiling and hugging him like the opposing pitcher's parents. He couldn't help but think how one hit would have changed everything.

Luke kept his baseball glove under his bed year-round. He liked keeping his glove in a place where he could reach it. Most of the time, he reached for it to play the sport he loved. However, there were nights when he grabbed his glove for reasons that didn't really involve baseball.

Sometimes, while lying in his bed, Luke could hear his parents arguing in their bedroom. He'd listen to their words, stare up at his bedroom wall, and find it hard to sleep. It was on such nights that Luke would reach to the floor, grab his glove, and hold it for the night. Whenever he put the glove on his chest, Luke would feel a peace that helped him relax. When he closed his eyes, he would have remarkable dreams that always involved baseball.

One night, he dreamed he was pitching to Babe Ruth. In this dream, Luke waited for the New York Yankees legend to point at the outfield with his bat before Luke struck him out. In another dream, Luke hit a home run to win the championship game for his Little League baseball team. One dream that kept coming back to Luke found him standing at the edge of a field. He'd hold a stick in one hand, toss a stone into the air with the other, and hit the stone with the stick. Over and over, Luke would pick up a stone, toss it up, and use the branch like a bat to hit it. Of all the dreams, this was the one Luke liked the best. There was no one else around in this dream. There was no game to be won. It was just Luke practicing his swing.

A baseball bat could always be found in the corner of Luke's room too. Baseballs seemed to roll freely in and out of the closet without any help. It was the way Luke Tyson liked his room. From the time he fell asleep to the second he woke up, baseball was never far from his eyes or heart.

Tonight Luke held his glove. He rolled over in his bed, lying on his side and staring at a patch of moonlight that had slipped through his window. The moonlight struck a baseball lying on the floor. Luke stared at the baseball, which seemed to be glowing in the darkness. He thought about the game, the missed hit, and his parents.

Luke pulled up his covers, took hold of his glove, and waited. He closed his eyes, hoping that something good would come to him in his dreams— something that would make him feel better.

THE CAGE

The next morning, Luke woke up when the sun was gold and not quite high enough in the sky to chase away the cool night air. Pulling a wagon, he walked two blocks from his house where he found a stack of newspapers waiting for him. Luke picked up the pile, carefully placed it into his wagon, and then began to walk his route.

It was his routine for the summer. While other kids were still in bed, Luke delivered papers to start the day. Since his father had lost his job, Luke decided he wanted to do his part for the family. The money didn't help his family a lot, but it was enough for Luke to pay for things he needed for the summer. That way he didn't have to ask his parents for money to go to the swimming pool or buy new socks for baseball. And Luke used some of the money to get better at baseball.

Pulling his wagon, tossing newspapers onto porches or into front yards, Luke thought about living in Hart County, Florida. There were very few parks with baseball fields in Hart, and those tended to be used by all the Little League baseball teams that made up the Florida Southern League. This meant that there were few chances for him to practice hitting, fielding, or pitching. This was one reason Luke needed the money.

Every morning Luke would finish his route by a stretch of sand called Santora Beach. Named after a Spanish explorer, the beach had small shops and plenty of white sand where people could spread out their towels for the day. There was also a story to Santora Beach, a story Luke was told at an early age.

A long time ago, long before America was a country, Diego Santora was exploring the Florida coast for the king of Spain. He commanded a ship filled with brave men who guarded the treasures they had found on their journey to America. Suddenly, a storm came over the sea and struck Santora's ship, breaking it in two. While the crew managed to swim to the beach, the treasures they were guarding simply vanished in the rough waters that pounded the shore.

Over the years, a few pieces of gold had turned up on Santora Beach. Luke heard stories about people digging in the sand and finding a piece or two. He knew some folks in Hart believed in a great treasure hidden on the beach, waiting to be found.

Every morning after delivering his papers, Luke would walk home by way of Santora Beach. He would pull his wagon past the shops and food stands scattered along a path next to the beach, beyond the volleyball players and joggers. Then he'd stop in front of the one thing that drew him there—a batting cage.

For a small price, Luke was able to pick up a bat, slip on a helmet, and spend a few minutes practicing his swing. Before entering the batting cage, Luke would adjust his batting helmet. He'd pick out just the right bat. He'd take a practice swing. Then he'd step into the cage. He'd look at the plate and find a spot where he felt comfortable. He'd take one more practice swing. Then he'd pop a token into the machine and wait for the first ball to hit.

Luke would keep notes on how many hits he made on each visit. He also kept a record of the ones he missed, along with notes on why he missed them—whether he had thought about something else for a split second, heard some noise right before his swing, or saw something move out of the corner of his eye.

All in all, this was the morning routine at Santora Beach. While some folks came for the beach and a few came looking for treasure, Luke came for the love of baseball.

"Morning, Luke," Dutch Howard said to Luke this morning. Dutch owned and operated the batting cage. He was an older man whose face was always tan and cracked in different places when he smiled. His hair was pure white and always cut short. He leaned out the window of his booth and looked at Luke. "How many swings you gonna be taking this morning?"

"I'll just take one token today," Luke said, digging change out of his pocket and handing it to Dutch.

"Here you go," Dutch said, handing Luke one token for the batting cage. When Dutch grinned, his one gold tooth caught the sunlight, causing Luke to squint. Then Dutch spoke the same words he always said to Luke: "Hope you hit a homer."

Luke pulled his wagon over to the batting cage. He found a helmet that fit just right. He picked up a bat and took a practice swing, but it felt too heavy. He found another bat, took a swing, and then put it down too. The last bat he picked up felt just right. Luke put the token into the pitching machine, stepped in, and waited for the first ball.

He heard the machine hum, noticed the pitching arm turn, and watched the first ball appear. Luke took a swing and missed. He looked down at his feet, changed his stance, and looked up to see another ball flying toward him. Luke swung again and this time hit the ball with part of the bat. He looked down and noticed his feet were too far apart. He adjusted them. Then he looked up to see another ball appear. This one Luke hit, and it flew against the netting behind the batting machine. In all, Luke hit two more balls and missed the others. Not his best,

Luke thought, but he did have three solid hits off pretty fast pitches. When he was finished, Luke stood in the cage for a minute and made a few more practice swings. Then he took his notebook out of his pocket and wrote some notes about his session before he forgot.

As he was leaving the cage, Luke noticed an older man watching him. He was tall and thin with dark skin. The man wore a bright blue suit and a black baseball cap. He tipped his cap to Luke and then turned and walked away. Luke thought he was probably just a bored old man walking along the beach. Luke grabbed the handle of his wagon and headed for home.

When he got home, Luke pulled his wagon into the garage. As he turned to head inside, he noticed something inside the wagon. It was a folded newspaper. Luke quickly retraced his route in his mind. He thought back to each house he visited, but he couldn't remember missing any of them.

"Someone's gonna be mad," Luke mumbled to himself.

He scooped up the paper, held it in the morning light, and noticed that it was the sports section of the Hart Daily News. Luke also noticed that in the top corner, the date of the paper was December 1982. While it was the newspaper he delivered, it was an old copy—from before he was born!

"How did this get here?" Luke wondered aloud.

He scanned the headlines from stories that were more than 20 years old. He saw stories about hockey, basketball, and boxing, but none of them interested Luke. Then his eyes stopped on a headline about baseball. It had been circled in black ink.

"Baseball hero remembered ten years later," Luke read.

The article was a series of memories about a baseball player named Roberto Clemente. Luke knew he was one of baseball's greats, but he didn't know many details about his life or career. He read the article.

Roberto had been born in Puerto Rico and had played for the Pittsburgh Pirates. He won the National League batting title four times. He received 12 Gold Glove awards for being so good at playing in right field. It was the same position Luke played, but that seemed to be the only thing they had in common. Unlike Luke, Roberto Clemente helped his team win two championships. Luke just wanted to help his team win a game.

The article also talked about what a good person Roberto Clemente was off the baseball field. He helped people who needed it, and he spent his own money building places where children in Puerto Rico could learn to play baseball. Then the article said that Roberto Clemente had died, but it didn't say how. The article simply talked about Roberto's work on and off the baseball field. It ended with a quote from Roberto Clemente himself. "Anytime you have an opportunity to make things better and you don't, then you are wasting your time on this Earth."

Luke put the paper down as two questions ran through his mind. Who put the paper in his wagon? And why?

As the day went by, Luke couldn't wait to get to baseball practice. Although Luke dreaded the spotlight of games when he seemed to let everyone down, he loved practice, where there was little pressure and he could just play ball.

When his father stopped the car at the park that evening for practice, Luke hopped out, gave his dad a quick wave, and then scanned the park to see which field his team had reserved. It was easy to find his team because of their blue baseball caps with the letter H in bright blue on the front.

"Hey, Luke!" a voice called out.

Luke scanned the dugout bench to see Thad waving him over. He ran over to his best friend. Luke and Thad were far from being the best players on the team. In fact, Luke thought they were probably the two worst. As they waited for the coach to arrive,

16

Luke told Thad about the batting cage and the newspaper that was left in his wagon.

"So how old was the paper?" Thad asked.

Luke described the paper to his friend. "I mean, this Clemente guy was a real good player. I just don't know why someone would have put the paper in my wagon."

"So you think it was the guy in the suit?" Thad asked.

"Guess so," Luke shrugged. "He was the only one close to the wagon."

"Then you gotta talk to him," Thad suggested. "Go back to the batting cage tomorrow and see if he's there."

"Coach wants us!" a voice called out.

The announcement caused Thad to jump off the bench and sprint for the field with the rest of his teammates. Luke slowly got up too and started jogging from the dugout. As he ran, he thought about what Thad had said. Luke's parents had warned him not to talk to strangers. It was one of the first rules they taught him when he was very young. Since his dad lost his job, Luke had been trying to do as many right things as possible. He knew it didn't take much for his parents to argue, so he decided not to give them a reason to get mad. Now Luke was going to break his parents' rule tomorrow at the beach. He knew he had to talk to the stranger.

THE STRANGER

The next morning began as always with Luke delivering his newspapers. After he'd finished, he pulled his wagon down to the beach and fished out some change for Dutch. Then he walked to the batting cage and slipped on a batting helmet.

As he selected a bat, Luke looked around at the people walking to and from Santora Beach. Most of them wore swimsuits. A few wore shirts. No one was wearing a suit or a baseball hat. Luke turned his attention to the batting cage. He dropped his token into the machine and then stepped up to the plate.

When the machine began to hum, Luke saw the first pitch appear and fly at him. He swung and missed. The next pitch was a little lower, but Luke swung high and missed again. In between each pitch, Luke's eyes glanced outside the cage for the man in the suit. Perhaps that was why he only got three hits out of ten for his token. When he was finished, Luke started to put his helmet and bat away when he heard a voice say, "Three hundred."

"Huh?" Luke replied. He turned and was surprised to see that it was the stranger from yesterday. He noticed that the man was wearing a brown suit this time but the same black baseball cap. Luke watched as the man took off the cap, scratched his curly gray hair, and smiled. He put the black cap back on and walked up to where Luke was standing.

"You hit three out of ten," the man observed. "That means you're batting .300. It's a pretty good average for a baseball player."

"Thanks," Luke said, hanging up his batting helmet and putting down the bat.

"You're swinging too hard, though," the man continued. "Keep your arms loose. Relax your hands."

"Are you a baseball coach or something?" Luke finally asked.

"Nope," the man answered, "just someone who knows a lot about baseball."

"Oh," Luke mumbled, "thanks for the tip." Luke paused, wanting to ask him about the paper but losing his nerve. "I gotta get going."

"You hit five out of ten the day before yesterday," the man continued. "That morning your swing was looser. You got out in front of the pitches a little better."

"You were watching me?" Luke asked.

"I take a walk here every morning," the man replied. "I just happen to walk by when you're here. So why do you hit baseballs every morning?"

" 'Cause I want to be the best," Luke replied.

"Really?" the man asked, tilting his head to one side. "I've heard a lot of baseball players say the same thing. You know what I tell them? I say it's a long road to being the best at something, especially baseball."

"What do you mean?"

"Well," the man began, "let's take your team. Let's say you're the best one on your team. The next step would be for you to become the best in your league. After that, you'd have to become the best in the state, and then if you're real good and real lucky, the best player in the major leagues. Like I said . . . it's a long road to travel when you want to be the best."

"I see," Luke managed to answer.

"I've known plenty of baseball players who have tried to be the best," the man observed. "You sure you really want to go down that road?"

"I gotta go, Mister," Luke said, avoiding the question and reaching down for the handle to his wagon.

"Call me, Sonny," the man smiled. "Sonny Garcia."

"Luke," Luke said, introducing himself too. Luke knew he probably shouldn't be telling a stranger his name, but something told him he could trust this guy.

"So now that you know my name," said Mr. Garcia, "tell me, why do you come here pulling a wagon?"

"Paper route," Luke answered. He wasn't sure how much to tell Mr. Garcia. He seemed nice enough, but Luke reminded himself that he didn't really know anything about the man. "Look, Mr. Garcia, it was nice to meet you, but I gotta go."

"Here," Mr. Garcia said, sticking something in Luke's hand. "Maybe this will help you remember that tip I was talking about."

Luke looked in his hand to find a baseball card. On the front of the card was a picture of Roberto Clemente. He looked young in the picture, Luke thought. He turned the card over and noticed that Roberto had only been playing for a few seasons. He also saw that there was a small article written about the player. Luke noticed there was one part of the article underlined. He held up the card and read the underlined part. "Roberto is one of the best hitters in baseball. He does not swing for home runs. This is one reason Roberto has won a batting title and should win many more before he retires," Luke read out loud. He looked up to see that Mr. Garcia had walked away.

The edges of the card were worn. He flipped the card over and looked at the picture. The picture had small creases and the colors were faded. He guessed it must have been a very old baseball card. Where did Mr. Garcia come across a card like this? Why did he choose this card and this player?

When he returned home, Luke forgot about Mr. Garcia and Roberto Clemente for a while. Luke found his father sitting at the kitchen table. As had been the routine for the last few months, his father kept one hand on a steaming mug of coffee. His eyes stared down at the morning paper spread out on the table. His other hand held a pen that he used to circle job ads.

Three months ago Luke's dad came home and said he had been "let go" by the car company he'd worked for since before Luke was born. He'd been helping the company build cars for years. Luke found out that his dad was one of many people that the company decided they didn't need. That's when Luke's mom got her job at a nearby restaurant. She promised Luke it would only be for "a little while." Long enough for Luke's dad to find a job. Three months, and nearly a hundred newspapers later, Luke's dad was still searching for some kind of work.

"How was your newspaper route?" Luke's dad asked while he read.

"Okay," Luke answered.

"You got a game tomorrow?" Luke's dad began, his eyes leaving his paper. Luke watched his father reach down and pull up a baseball glove. "Wanna catch a few?"

"Let me get my glove," Luke said, sprinting to his room.

When he opened the door, Luke dove under his bed for his glove. He also picked up a baseball that was lying on the floor next to his closet. Then he charged back down the steps and into the kitchen where his father was waiting.

Luke and his father went into the backyard, which was narrow but long. Fences divided both sides of the yard from their neighbors' properties. Luke ran down to the end of the yard and then turned in time to see his father make the first throw. It was a time that Luke liked the best. It was quiet. It was fun. It was just the two of them.

"This will be your fifth game . . . right?" Luke's dad asked.

"Yes, sir," Luke answered, throwing the ball back.

"How many hits have you had so far?"

"None," Luke answered a bit more quietly.

"That's right," his dad nodded, "still looking for that first one."

"Yes, sir," Luke quickly said. "I got a feeling I'll get one tomorrow."

"That's good," his dad replied. He wound up and softly tossed the ball into Luke's glove.

"Dad," Luke began, "you find any jobs in the paper today?"

"A couple," Luke's dad replied. "Made a few phone calls. Might have an interview lined up. Just gotta take things as they come, Luke. Don't worry. You just think about getting yourself a hit tomorrow."

"I will," Luke answered.

"Try to remember to stay calm," Luke's dad suggested. "I think maybe you try a little too hard sometimes when you're at the plate. Stay relaxed and have fun."

24

"I'll try," Luke answered. Luke's dad always told him to relax and have fun before a game. Luke always promised to take his advice. Yet, deep down, Luke knew he couldn't relax. He knew he had to be the best. He knew that he couldn't tell his father why, but he knew he had to play better in every game.

4

A SHOP

BY THE SEA

The next morning Luke delivered his papers a little faster. He was in a hurry to get back to Santora Beach and the batting cage. He wanted to get in some good practice for the evening's game. He was also interested in seeing if Mr. Garcia would be there.

When he arrived, Luke went over to the booth by the batting cage and gave his money to Dutch. While Dutch counted the coins and fished out a token, Luke looked over to see Mr. Garcia walking down the beach.

"Here you go," Dutch said, sliding the token over to Luke. "Hope you hit a homer, Luke."

"Who is that?" Luke asked, pointing to Mr. Garcia.

"Huh?" Dutch mumbled, squinting out at the beach. "Looks like old Sonny Garcia to me. Nice guy."

"He was giving me some tips on my swing yesterday," Luke said.

"Better listen to him," Dutch suggested. "Sonny used to be a baseball scout. Helped a whole bunch of talent get to the big leagues. If he tells you something, you'd be better off listening to him.

Maybe he sees something special in you."

"Why is he always hanging around here?" Luke asked.

"He's got a sports shop not far from here," Dutch said.

Luke turned to see Mr. Garcia walking to the batting cage. He was wearing a long-sleeved white shirt, long black pants, and a matching black hat. He was dressed very differently than the other people who were wearing swimsuits and T-shirts.

"Morning, Luke," Mr. Garcia said as Luke walked up to the cage. "Fine morning for a walk."

"You've got to be hot in that," Luke said, pointing to the outfit. "Why do you get so dressed up for a walk?"

"I'm on my way to work," Mr. Garcia said. "Mind if I watch you hit a few?"

"Why me?" Luke asked. "There must be other people who use these batting cages. Why don't you watch them?"

"You're right," Mr. Garcia nodded. "I see a few people come here and pay money to hit baseballs. You're the only one who comes every day. You're the only one who looks like it's more than just fun. You look like it's . . . important."

Luke turned his eyes to the racks of batting helmets and bats that lined the outside of the cage. He grabbed a blue helmet and a shiny aluminum bat. Then he slipped his coin into the machine for his ten pitches. He stepped into the batting cage, adjusted his feet next to the plate, and waited for his chances.

The first three pitches were hard and a little high. Luke found himself swinging his bat a little harder than yesterday. He missed on all three swings. Then he hit one that came in a little lower and not as fast. It was a solid hit, causing his hands to feel a slight sting from the bat. He connected on two more before missing his last four.

Three hits, just like yesterday, Luke thought. Part of the problem, he told himself, was that Mr. Garcia was watching him. Though he wasn't in Luke's view, he was still a distraction. Luke knew he was right behind him, and after his last swing, he turned around to find Mr. Garcia smiling at him.

"So why are you here every morning?" Mr. Garcia asked.

"My baseball team hasn't won a game this season. I just want to play my best so I can help my team win one," Luke said.

"The way you hit in this batting cage, you must be one of the better players on your team," Mr. Garcia observed.

Luke paused for a minute and looked at Mr. Garcia. "Truth is, I've never been very good at anything, Mr. Garcia. Never won anything. I'm not the fastest in school. Heck, I'm not even the strongest in my gym class. I know I'm not the smartest in my classes. I don't get straight A's like some of the brains at my school. Guess I figure baseball is gonna be my best chance to be good at something. Maybe that's why I come here every morning. The way I figure it, baseball is my best chance to make them happy."

"Who's them?" Mr. Garcia asked.

"Never mind," Luke sighed, refusing to talk about his parents. He liked Mr. Garcia, but he wasn't ready to tell him about what was going on with his family.

"I see," Mr. Garcia said. He looked at Luke, nodded, and then turned his eyes to the batting cage. "Well at least you're consistent. You got three hits yesterday and three more today."

"Could have done better," Luke answered. "I think my bat was a little too heavy. It wasn't as easy to swing." Luke took his notebook out of his pocket and jotted down his assessment of today's hits and misses.

"You're right," Mr. Garcia nodded. "I could tell your bat was heavy for you."

"How did you know?" Luke asked.

"Your swing," Mr. Garcia pointed out. "You weren't as quick with the bat. It was slower off your shoulder, and you didn't have great control. Your swing was not very even. You still have that card I gave you?"

"Yeah," Luke answered, fishing it out of his backpack in his wagon.

"Gotta keep your arms loose," Mr. Garcia advised, pointing at the card. "That's what Roberto Clemente used to do."

"What made Roberto Clemente so special?" Luke asked, looking at the card.

"Roberto Clemente was one of the greatest players ever," Mr. Garcia stated. "He played for the Pittsburgh Pirates. He won the batting championship four times and finished his career averaging three hits for every ten at bats. That's a .300 batting average, Luke, and that's not bad. That's kind of the way you've been hitting the last couple of mornings."

"How do you know so much about Roberto Clemente?" Luke asked.

"It has been a hobby of mine," Mr. Garcia said. "When you own a sports shop, you learn all kinds of things."

"What kind of sports stuff do you sell?" Luke asked.

"If you're done here," Mr. Garcia said, "maybe you can come to my shop. I'll show you something very special that was given to me. Something that will answer your question about why I know so much about Roberto Clemente."

Luke thought about what Mr. Garcia was asking. He turned and looked back at Dutch. He noticed that

Dutch was watching them, then nodded to Luke as if to say it would be okay.

"Where is it?" Luke asked.

"Right over there," Mr. Garcia said, pointing to a small building in between a hot dog stand and a T-shirt shop. Luke nodded and followed Mr. Garcia.

"I never noticed this place before," Luke said. Even when they reached the front door to the shop, he could still see the batting cages. They paused while Mr. Garcia unlocked the door and then opened it for Luke to enter.

The inside was dark, with shafts of golden light shooting through the windows and striking the dark wood floor. It was also very hot, something Mr. Garcia quickly took care of by turning on the air conditioner behind the counter. Luke walked up to the counter and saw that it was actually a glass case. Inside the case, he saw autographed baseballs, old baseball caps, and ticket stubs with faded letters and dates from long before Luke was born.

Suddenly the store lights came on. Luke turned around to see large glass cases in the center of the room. Inside the cases hung old baseball jerseys with names like Brooklyn and Washington stitched onto them with fancy letters.

"I didn't know those places had baseball teams," Luke said.

"History of baseball is as deep as the ocean," Mr. Garcia said, digging behind the counter. "There's a

31

lot to learn. That's part of the fun of the game. Come here. Let me show you one treasure that really came from the ocean."

Luke wandered over to the counter and watched as Mr. Garcia put a long object on the counter. The object was wrapped with a blanket.

"This came with a story," Mr. Garcia recalled, resting his hand on the blanket.

"What is it?" Luke asked.

"A nice old man brought this in one day," Mr. Garcia explained. "He told me he lived near a beach called Isla Verde, which is in Puerto Rico. Many years ago, while he was walking along the beach, he saw a large group of people standing at the shore. He remembered seeing lots of planes flying over the ocean that morning. They circled like birds searching for something. That's when he heard someone say the planes were there because of an accident. That a plane had crashed the night before, and there were important people on the plane. Important people to be rescued."

"Did they find the people on the plane?" Luke asked.

"I'm afraid they didn't," Mr. Garcia replied. He scratched the gray whiskers sticking out on his chin. "The old man said he recalled how every person on the beach stood silent in prayer. How those who did speak ended their sentences by shaking their heads

32

when they spoke of the accident. He said they spoke of the brave people from America who crashed into the sea."

"Why were they brave?" Luke asked.

"The old man said they were brave because they had come to help people," Mr. Garcia recalled. "You see, there was a bad earthquake in Puerto Rico that year. A lot of people were hurt and needed help. The plane that crashed was bringing supplies from America. Help was coming because of one man— Roberto Clemente."

"A great baseball player," Luke recalled.

"Yes," Mr. Garcia smiled. "A great baseball player who was very proud of his home country, Puerto Rico. It was Roberto Clemente who had collected the supplies, and it was Roberto Clemente who wanted to deliver them."

"So he was on the plane?" Luke asked.

"I'm afraid he was," Mr. Garcia nodded.

"Then that's how he died," Luke said to himself, his eyes turning to the floor. He looked at Mr. Garcia. "Why are you telling me this?"

"As I said, this object came with a story," Mr. Garcia replied. He paused for a moment, clearing his throat and looking down at his hands.

"What?" Luke begged, now hanging on every word.

"Weeks went by and no plane was found," Mr. Garcia continued. "Folks just decided to get on with

33

things. The old man told me he went for a walk on the beach one morning. He remembered seeing this one white shell sparkle in the light. When he reached for it, a big wave came up, hit him at his knees, and almost knocked him to the ground. In trying to keep his balance, he noticed something wash up on the shore. Something long. Something he had never seen come from the sea."

"What was it?" Luke asked.

"A baseball bat," Mr. Garcia answered.

"So the old man said it was . . . from the plane?" Luke asked. "He thought the bat belonged to Roberto Clemente?"

"Now of course I don't know if it's true," Mr. Garcia began. "I've seen pictures of Roberto Clemente playing baseball. I've seen close-up photographs of the kind of bat he used. I have an idea of what it looked like."

"Do you believe him?" Luke asked.

"Yes," Mr. Garcia nodded.

Mr. Garcia's hands slowly began to open the blanket. What appeared from the blanket was something long and wooden. Something that caused Luke's eyes to grow wide.

"Is that the bat?" Luke asked.

Mr. Garcia nodded, sliding the bat across the counter.

It was made of wood, Luke thought. Most bats at the batting cage and used in Little League were made of aluminum. The wood was light in color. Long black lines stretched up along the wood's grain. Luke ran his hand over the bat. The surface felt smooth, and it looked shiny when the light struck it. He rolled the bat over and saw one very dark line running down the side of the bat, and he wondered if it was from the wood or from the plane crash.

"You can pick it up," Mr. Garcia said. "Go ahead, take a few swings with it. See if it feels as good as the bats you use in the batting cage."

Luke picked up the bat. He could feel the grain of wood in his hands. He took a few steps back from the counter, cocked the bat on his shoulder, and took an easy swing. The bat seemed to float through the air. He didn't need a lot of muscle to lift it or swing it. As he took another swing, Luke couldn't help but think that he might be swinging the same bat that had once belonged to Roberto Clemente. Luke closed his eyes, swung the bat, and thought he heard the sound of a crowd cheer for a split second.

"Did you hear that?" Luke asked, standing in the middle of the shop with the bat on his shoulder.

"Hear what?" Mr. Garcia replied, opening his cash register and looking down at its contents.

"Thought I . . . never mind," Luke said, too embarrassed to explain.

"It's the bat," Mr. Garcia said, reaching over the counter and taking it from Luke's hands. "Yes . . . there's something about this bat. Some kind of magic that it still holds. Look what it helped Roberto

35

Clemente do in the big leagues. I think there's still some magic left in it. Maybe that's what you heard, Luke. Maybe it was the magic talking to you."

"Or the ocean," Luke quickly added. He gave Mr. Garcia a polite smile and tried to ignore all his talk about a magic bat. "Thank you for letting me see your shop. You've got a lot of cool stuff."

"Good luck with your game," Mr. Garcia said. He wrapped the bat up in the cloth and put it away. "Remember . . . keep your arms relaxed."

As he walked home, Luke thought about the story Mr. Garcia had just told. He stopped and pulled out the card of Roberto from his backpack and looked at it. Then he placed it back inside his backpack so nothing would happen to it.

On his way home, Luke stopped in front of a restaurant called Sally's Diner. He pulled his wagon along the sidewalk and then paused in front of the large window to watch a slender woman waiting on tables. Her blond hair was pinned up high on her head. Luke watched her smile and nod to a group of men at a table. Luke waited for her to look out the window, but she was too busy writing down orders. Every so often Luke stopped at Sally's Diner to see his mom work as a waitress. It looked like hard work to Luke, but his mom always made it look easy.

Luke parked his wagon next to the front door. He carefully opened the door to Sally's Diner and walked inside.

"One grilled cheese on rye!" he heard a voice call out from the kitchen.

"Two dogs, no kraut, ready for pick up," another voice shouted.

Luke stood by the door, watching his mother smile and nod to the men at the table. While she did both, she continued to write down their orders on her small tablet. After writing down the last order, Luke watched her tuck the pen away, turn, and stop when she noticed Luke standing near the front door.

"Luke. What are you doing here?" his mom asked with a tired smile. Her cheeks were red and her face glowed with sweat. After a few seconds, the smile quickly faded. "Is there something wrong?"

"No," Luke quickly answered. "Just was heading home from my route and . . . I wanted to see you."

"That's sweet, Luke," his mom sighed, the smile returning to her face. She wrapped her arms around him and gave him a quick hug.

"Looks busy," Luke observed, turning to see people seated, talking and eating much faster than Luke ever could.

"It's lunchtime," Luke's mom replied. "That means it's a real busy time right now, so I really can't chitchat, sweetie. My boss is gonna get mad if I don't keep moving."

"That's okay," Luke answered. "Just wanted to see you on my way home."

"Got some orders stacking up!" a woman's voice yelled from behind the counter.

"Coming, Sally!" Luke's mom shouted back. Her eyes jumped to a table. She looked back at the kitchen and then quickly turned to Luke. "Gotta get going, Luke. You tell your dad I'll be home early today."

Before Luke could say another word, she gave him a quick smile, turned, and disappeared behind the counter to collect some more orders. Luke slowly walked out the door and then watched his mother through the window for a minute.

He watched her quickly move around tables while carrying four plates at once. He saw her serve some people with a smile. She poured water with one hand while clearing empty plates with the other. Then her eyes turned to Luke, which caused her to smile once more. She looked tired, Luke thought. He'd walked by her restaurant other days but never saw her look so tired. He knew she didn't like being a waitress, but she wanted to help them pay the bills. It was the reason she was working. It was the reason she fought with his father.

AN EASY SWING

During baseball games, Luke observed how much time was spent sitting in the dugout. Time spent waiting to go back out to the field. Time spent waiting for a turn to bat. Luke usually spent his time watching all the different ways that Coach Futz would fidget and move.

Coach Hank Futz was a big man. Luke wasn't sure if his arms had a round shape because of muscle or fat. Coach Futz's stomach, full and round, tended to shake when he walked around the baseball field. Luke also noticed that on the few times he broke into a slow trot, Coach Futz tended to take small steps and wobble like a bowling pin. Now a few weeks into the season, Luke knew all the ways his baseball coach moved and what parts tended to jiggle.

"Smack one out of the ballpark!" Coach Futz snorted to one of Luke's teammates.

The Hart Sharks were down by one run against the Stallions of Summit City. It was the Sharks' last time at bat, and Luke noticed that Coach Futz was tugging at the waistband of his pants. Luke knew that he always pulled up his pants when he was nervous. Every time he pulled them up, the pants would slide back down the slope of his rather large stomach.

"Luke!" he grunted. "You're up next!"

The words caught Luke's attention. He looked up to see Thad standing at the plate. Luke got up, walked over, and looked at the bats. He had tried three different bats during the game but had yet to get a hit. He looked at the choices, picked up one bat, and took a swing. It felt a little lighter than the other ones.

"Go Thad!" he heard Coach Futz shout.

Luke turned in time to see Thad sprinting to first base, only to lose out to a quick throw from the Stallions shortstop. Two outs. They were down by one run.

Luke turned his eyes to the bats, grabbed hold of a heavy one, and then took a swing.

"Get a hit, Luke," he heard a voice call out from the dugout.

"Wait for your pitch, Luke," Coach Futz advised.

Luke just nodded and walked out to the plate. He looked up at the Stallions pitcher on the mound. While he waited for the first pitch, he felt how tense his arms were holding up the heavy bat. He thought about Mr. Garcia's advice to keep his arms loose and wondered how he would manage to do that.

Luke swung at the first pitch, a low throw that almost hit the plate. Luke stepped back, took a deep breath, and then checked his feet as he moved back to the plate. He tried to stay relaxed even though he could hear his team yelling his name. Another throw went outside, and this time Luke didn't swing.

"Ball!" the umpire yelled.

Luke stayed next to the plate, kept his eyes on the pitcher, and took a practice swing with the heavy bat. He watched the pitcher throw a ball that looked like a perfect pitch to Luke. He stepped forward, swung the bat, and felt it vibrate as it launched the ball into the air. Luke dropped the bat and started to run, keeping his eye on the ball as it sailed into the outfield. He watched a Stallions player run under the ball, catch it, and then raise his arms into the air. The Stallions had won.

"Shoot!" Luke mumbled to himself, lowering his head and kicking the dirt. He turned around to see Coach Futz clapping his hands together and getting Luke's teammates out to shake hands with the Stallions' players. Luke looked over for his parents standing at the side of the field. He spotted his mom standing by herself, but he couldn't find his dad. He looked back at his mom. She smiled and blew him a kiss. Luke quickly smiled back, looking around to see if anyone on his team saw what his mom had just done. A quick scan of the field and he knew he was lucky. No one had noticed that his mom had just totally embarrassed him.

"Gave it your best shot," Coach Futz growled when Luke returned to the dugout. "Just got under it a little too much."

"Yeah," Luke said, putting his helmet down and the bat away.

"We'll get a win next time," Coach Futz said. It was what Coach Futz always said after a loss. Whether they lost by one run or by ten runs,

Coach Futz never had anything new to say. Never got mad. He always said with the same straight face that they'd "get" the next game.

As Luke walked over to where his mom was standing, he noticed someone standing behind home plate. The man was wearing a brown suit, a black baseball cap, and a friendly smile. It was Mr. Garcia. Luke wanted to wave at him, but he knew his mom was watching. If he went over to Mr. Garcia, then his mom would start asking questions. She'd find out he had been going to the beach in the mornings. Luke didn't think his parents would approve of him going to the beach by himself. Still, Luke wanted to keep going because of the batting cage. He wanted to keep getting better. It was all part of the plan. He flashed Mr. Garcia a quick smile and kept walking toward his mom.

"Where's Dad?" Luke asked.

"He had to meet with someone about a job," his mom replied.

"But it's getting dark," Luke said, bouncing his glove on his knee.

"He was going to try to make it," she said. "Maybe the meeting went well."

While Luke followed his mother to the car, she talked about how much better things would be if his dad got a job. All Luke could think about was that he hadn't gotten a hit. He needed to play better. He could hit three out of ten balls at the batting cage, but he'd just gone through his fifth game without getting a hit. He needed to play better. He needed to do it for his parents.

THE BAT

The next morning Luke woke with his glove in his arms. As he rolled onto his side, he remembered what he'd heard the night before. His mother's voice complaining about his father not being at the baseball game. His father's voice explaining why. His mother's voice pressing him to find a job. His father's voice getting defensive, saying he was doing everything he could.

All of these words were followed by silence. It was the kind of silence that Luke knew was filled with anger. Sometimes Luke would get quiet after a fight with a friend, only to think about what had made him so mad. He wondered if his parents were thinking about their words when they finally went to sleep.

He also wondered why they had to fight. He thought about it when he picked up his newspapers. He thought about it as he walked his route. He thought about it on the way to Santora Beach. Didn't they still love each other? Would the fights get worse?

"Morning, Dutch," Luke said, handing him some coins.

"Morning, Luke," Dutch replied, sliding a token across the counter.

Luke was making his way to the batting cage when he saw Mr. Garcia standing next to the cage. This morning he wore a blue suit with a matching cap and a smile. Luke also noticed that Mr. Garcia had something tucked under his arm—something that was long and wooden.

"I saw your game," Mr. Garcia said. "You made some good plays, but you had some problems at the plate. Your swing was just a little . . . off."

"That's why I'm here," Luke said, slipping on a batting helmet. He picked up a bat and took a few practice swings.

"How long you gonna keep coming back here?" Mr. Garcia asked.

"Long as I got a paper route," Luke answered.

"Still want to get better?" Mr. Garcia asked.

"I've got to," Luke softly answered.

"And it's still important?" Mr. Garcia asked.

"More than you know," Luke said, thinking about his parents.

"I see," Mr. Garcia sighed. His eyes looked down at the ground. He pressed his lips together and looked at Luke.

"Of course it would take a miracle for me to get good. Least that's what the guys on the team say to me," Luke said.

"So that's what they say," Mr. Garcia smiled. "I like you, Luke. You care about baseball more than most grown-ups. It's the one thing you want to be better at than most people. I think someone who loves baseball as much as you deserves a miracle."

With that last word, Luke watched Mr. Garcia hold the bat that he had been carrying under his arm up in the air. He held it tight with both hands, looked at it, and smiled at the bat like it was a long lost friend.

Then Luke noticed the dark black line down the side of the bat.

"Is that the bat you showed me? Is that Roberto's bat?" Luke asked.

"It served Clemente well," Mr. Garcia said. "Maybe it still has some magic left in it for one more season. We'll never know if we leave it in a glass case." He presented the bat to Luke.

Luke held the bat in both his hands and looked closely at it. He studied every line, every shade, every grain of wood. The bat felt cool and smooth in his hands.

"Are you sure?" Luke asked. "I mean . . . what if it breaks or cracks?"

"It survived hundred-mile-an-hour pitches, a plane crash, and a stormy sea," Mr. Garcia said. "I think it'll hold together for you."

Luke grabbed the handle of the bat. He pulled the bat up into position and took a practice swing.

It felt as light as the wind. He looked at the bat again. Then he thought of something that made his heart race. He was holding a bat that was once used by a major league baseball player. He had just swung a bat that used to be swung by Roberto Clemente!

In his mind, Luke could see Roberto, dressed in his black-and-gold uniform, getting a hit with the bat and sprinting to first base. Luke was tingling from head to toe.

"Go ahead," Mr. Garcia said, pointing to the cage. "Let's see if it's still got some hits left in it."

Luke stepped into the cage. He slipped a token into the machine, walked back to the plate, and gently rested the bat on his shoulder. He heard the pitching machine begin to hum, lifted his bat slightly, and he waited for the first ball to fly at him.

"Don't swing hard," Luke told himself.

The first ball flew at him. Luke watched it close in on the plate. Suddenly the bat moved, his arms swung, and he made solid contact with the ball. The next ball came low. Luke bent his knees and hit the ball right back at the machine. Two more pitches were high and hard, but Luke somehow managed to swing high and connect on both pitches. Three more pitches produced three more hits. Luke couldn't believe it. He looked at the bat for a second and then hit another pitch high and behind the pitching machine. One pitch came in close to Luke, but he managed to step back, swing, and still hit it. Another pitch was right down the center of the plate, and Luke sent it bouncing back up the middle of the cage. The machine grew silent. The balls stopped flying. Luke remained at the plate.

"Ten hits," Luke said to himself.

"You were perfect," Mr. Garcia said from behind.

"What?" Luke asked, still lost in the moment.

"Ten for ten," Mr. Garcia smiled. "That's your best morning yet, Luke. You sure had a sweet swing for all those pitches. Nice and loose . . . and perfect."

"Thanks," Luke said, stepping out of the cage. He started to take off his helmet when Mr. Garcia rushed up to him.

"Wait!" Mr. Garcia said sharply. He was holding out his hand and waving something in it. "I have another token. Let's try a harder batting cage and see how you do." He pointed to a batting cage where most grown-ups went to practice their hitting. The machine threw the balls harder than Luke was used to hitting.

"But no one in my league throws the ball that hard," Luke remarked. Part of him didn't want to go into the cage because he was afraid of the speed that the balls were being pitched. Yet, something made him feel a little daring this morning. Something made him feel a little brave.

"I'll give it a try," Luke said, walking over to the next cage.

When he reached the cage, he had to wait for a tall man with long blond hair to finish. Luke listened as the man swung at each pitch. His swing was quick, and Luke could hear the man grunt whenever he missed the ball. After a few more swings, the man was finished. He slipped on his sunglasses, flashed Luke a frustrated smile, and sighed.

"Good luck, kid!"

Luke adjusted the helmet on his head. He rubbed the bat with his hands, wondering what was going to happen.

"You ready?" Mr. Garcia asked.

"I guess," Luke said, feeling a little nervous.

Mr. Garcia handed Luke a token to put into the machine and then moved back and nodded. Luke dropped the token into the machine, stepped up to the plate, and heard the machine begin to hum. He took a practice swing with the bat. His arms were loose. He felt strangely calm.

The first pitch came right at him. Luke stepped back and caught the ball early with his bat. The next two pitches were low and hard, but somehow Luke's bat managed to connect with both of them. Three more pitches came right down the middle so fast that Luke could barely see them, yet he managed to hit them clean and right back up the middle. Then Luke took the last four pitches, all high and hard, and nailed them straight back to the netting behind the machine.

The machine stopped. The sunlight poured down from behind a cloud. Luke turned to see Mr. Garcia grinning. He also saw a group of grown-ups standing around Mr. Garcia, also staring at Luke with smiles on their faces. Everyone in attendance, even Luke, knew they had seen something special. A few even clapped. Luke just looked at the bat and tried to make sense of it all.

On the way to practice that afternoon, Luke's dad said, "Sorry about missing your game, Luke. I got caught in traffic after my meeting. I was thinking about you the whole time. Your mom said you almost won the game."

"Almost," Luke mumbled. He looked out the window and thought about asking his dad if he and his mom were getting a divorce. He remembered their argument last night. Part of him wanted to ask the question, but he was afraid of the answer.

"I'll be at your next game, Luke. I promise."

"I know," Luke said, his eyes looking ahead to the baseball field.

"So are you mad?"

"No," Luke mumbled. "Just really anxious to get to practice."

"Gonna give your new bat a try?" his dad asked.

"Maybe," Luke answered.

"And where did you get your bat again?" his dad asked.

"Found it on my route," Luke said.

"Don't see a whole lot of people using wooden baseball bats today," his dad observed.

"Guess not," Luke answered.

"I can't wait to see you use it," Luke's dad said. At the field, he stopped the car, reached into the backseat, and handed the bat to Luke. "Have a good practice."

As Luke walked toward the field, he could hear the familiar "ping" sound made when an aluminum bat hit a baseball. It was the same sound he heard at the start of every practice. All the players knew Coach Futz liked to start practice by giving each

player a turn to grab a bat and work on hitting.
With each ping he heard, Luke gripped his bat a
little tighter as he got closer to the field. The sound
also made him walk a little faster. When he reached
the dugout, he saw that most of his teammates
were on the field already. Coach Futz stood on the
mound lobbing balls over the plate.

Luke turned to the dugout to see Mark Grace
standing with a bat in his hands. Mark was a little
older than everyone else on the team. He was also
the tallest player on the team. Perhaps it was
because of his age and his height that Mark was the
unofficial captain of the team.

"Hey, Luke," Mark said, taking a quick swing
with his bat. "Bring your own bat?"

"Yeah," Luke said, digging through some
helmets until he found one that fit.

"Coach is mad about the game," Mark said.
"Told us we didn't get enough hits. Said all we're
gonna do today is batting practice."

"Grace!" Coach Futz barked. "You're up. I wanna
see you hit the cover off the ball. Luke, you're up
next!"

Luke stepped up from the dugout and watched
Coach Futz pitch to Mark Grace. The first pitch was
low, and Mark hit it on the ground to first base
where Brian Mason scooped it up in his glove. Mark
swung and missed on the next few pitches. Luke

watched as Mark pounded his bat into the plate, took a practice swing, and then stood with the bat on his shoulder, waiting for another pitch.

While he watched, Luke tried to stay relaxed. He reminded himself to do what Mr. Garcia had told him. He would try to keep his arms loose. He would not grip the bat too tightly. He would keep his eye on the ball and pretend he was back in the batting cage just taking some swings. He would try not to think about the fact that he was using Roberto's bat.

"Luke!" Coach Futz called out. "You're up!"

Luke walked up to the plate. As he moved from the on-deck circle, he passed Mark. He noticed how Mark was mumbling something to himself and staring at the ground. When Luke stepped up to the plate, he looked around to see all of his teammates standing in their positions in the field. Some of them stood with arms folded, not expecting Luke to get a hit. Coach Futz stood tall on the pitcher's mound. Luke watched as Coach Futz tugged on the waistband of his pants.

"Okay, Luke, just some nice easy pitches," Coach Futz announced. He took a deep breath. Then he leaned back to the point that Luke thought he was going to fall off the mound. That's when Luke saw a slow pitch fly toward the plate.

CRACK!

The ball fired off his bat and bounced off the mound, causing Coach Futz to nearly fall down. Luke watched the ball roll into the outfield for what would be a hit in any league. He heard some of his teammates giggle at Coach Futz's fast footwork on the mound.

"Nice hit," Coach Futz said. "Next pitch is gonna be a little harder."

Luke watched Coach Futz adjust his pants around his stomach before leaning back and throwing a pitch that was a little faster than the last one.

CRACK!

The bat launched the ball high into the air and out toward left field. Luke watched as Max Abel, the fastest player on the team, sprinted as hard as he could, only to see the ball sail over his head. Luke heard a couple people cheer his name after that hit. He knew that no one on his team had hit a home run this season. Seeing one in practice was as close as they had gotten to the real thing.

The next few pitches were about the same speed, and Luke made good contact on every one. Some hits dropped into the outfield. Some hits rolled through the infield.

One hit was another high shot that flew over Max Abel's head again. Luke never knew there were so many different ways to get hits.

After about ten pitches, Luke felt as if he were in complete control. He could spot a place in the field where no one was standing, take a swing, and watch the ball go right where he wanted it. In a way, Luke thought, it was as if the bat were reading his mind, seeing what kind of hit he wanted and then making it happen. Luke managed to hit every pitch that Coach Futz could throw.

"All right," Coach Futz said, rubbing his shoulder. He looked at Luke and gave him a big smile. It was the first smile he'd seen Coach Futz give all season. "Grab your glove and hit the outfield. Tim Conner, your turn to take some swings."

Luke ran back to the dugout and stuck his bat under the bench with his bag. He stopped for a minute, ran his hand over the wood grain, and smiled. Was it the bat? Was it the "magic" Mr. Garcia kept talking about? Maybe it was just because he'd been practicing so much. Whatever the reason, Luke had stood at the plate and managed to hit the best throws Coach Futz could give him. Luke grabbed his glove and jogged to the field.

"That was so cool," he heard Mark Grace say as he passed him at first base. "Where'd you learn to hit like that?"

"Just been practicing," Luke replied. He slipped on his glove and stopped in the outfield. Thad, playing center field, ran over to Luke with a big grin on his face.

"Man, Luke," Thad laughed, "you almost whacked the coach. Then you hit two over Max's head, and he's the fastest guy on the team! How'd you do that?"

"It was that guy," Luke said. "The guy at the batting cage."

"What did he do . . . give you some tips?" Thad asked.

"Something like that," Luke replied. He wanted to tell Thad about the bat, but he didn't want it to get around. If his team found out that his bat had once belonged to a major-league baseball player, they'd all want to use it. Even worse, Luke thought, someone might want to steal it. Besides, if they knew he thought the bat contained some secret magic, Luke would be laughed off the team.

7
THE DREAM

The next morning Luke decided it was time to
share his stories about the batting cage and batting
practice with his parents. He started the moment he
set foot in the kitchen and continued when he sat
down. While he spoke, Luke noticed how his parents
reacted to each detail. His father sat with his mouth
wide open, nodding after every sentence. His mother
offered a smaller smile from behind her cup of coffee.

They gave an abbreviated version of the "you-should-have-asked-before-going-to-the-beach-by-yourself" speech and then listened as Luke relayed the rest of his story.

"And then at practice," Luke stated, "I hit two home runs. I mean, I hit them so hard, they flew over everyone's heads. Then I got a hit that went right past Coach Futz. He threw his hardest pitch, and I was still able to hit it."

"That's great, Luke," his dad nodded. He looked at Luke's mom and smiled. "Isn't that great, honey?"

"Yes, it is," Luke's mom said with a more controlled smile. She put her coffee mug down. "Well, I hope you hit a home run today."

"Thanks, Mom," Luke replied. "So, Dad, do you think we could throw some this afternoon? Maybe practice a little before the game?"

"Sure," his dad answered.

"I thought you had a job interview today," Luke's mom said.

"I know," Luke's dad nodded, "I'll have time to do both."

"It's okay, Dad. No big deal," Luke said. He got up from the kitchen table. He grabbed his bat and walked out the back door for his wagon. When he stepped out onto the porch, he could barely hear the sound of his parents' voices. They were growing louder when he stepped off the porch.

As he started his paper route, Luke tried not to think about what might have happened between his parents when he left them. He couldn't remember the last time he'd heard them argue during the day, and he was afraid it was a sign that things were getting worse between them. If they started to fight both night and day, Luke thought, then they might start using the word *divorce*. Now more than ever, he needed to get to the batting cage. Now more than ever, he needed to give them something to be happy about. Now was the time he needed to do something special on the baseball field.

"Morning, Luke," Dutch Howard grinned after Luke had finished delivering his papers. The wrinkles on his face curved every which way around his smile. "Quite a show you put on the other day. Never saw anyone hit the ball the way you did in that batting cage. Guess old Sonny Garcia must be giving you some good tips."

"Yeah," Luke nodded, handing Dutch some money. "He really knows a lot about baseball. He talks a lot about Roberto Clemente."

"Clemente was somethin' else," Dutch said. "I saw him play once. He had a knack for finding the right place to hit the ball. Could steal a base in a blink. Yeah, I remember Clemente. He was real good."

While he listened to Dutch go on about his memories of Roberto Clemente, Luke held the bat in both hands. He gripped it tightly. He couldn't wait to get in the batting cage to see how many hits he could get today.

"Hope you hit a home run," Dutch said, finally handing Luke his token.

When Luke reached the batting cage, he grabbed a helmet and quickly stepped up to the plate. He took a couple of practice swings and was about to put his token in the machine when he heard a voice ask, "Gonna waste the magic?"

Luke turned around to see Mr. Garcia standing outside the cage. This morning he was back in his dark suit and black baseball cap.

"Hi, Mr. Garcia," Luke said.

"I see you brought the bat," Mr. Garcia said.

"Yeah," Luke nodded. "What was that you said before?"

"I asked if you were gonna waste the magic," Mr. Garcia said.

"What do you mean?" Luke asked.

"A baseball player knows that a bat only has so many hits in it," Mr. Garcia said. "Maybe you'd be better off saving that bat for your games. I mean . . . you don't want to waste any hits in a batting cage, do you?"

"It's just a bat," Luke quickly answered. "Besides, maybe I can do better than yesterday. You know, get more hits in the fastest batting cage."

"Where do you want to be the best?" Mr. Garcia asked. "In the batting cage or on the baseball field?"

"The baseball field, I guess," Luke said, lowering the bat from his shoulder.

"All right, then," Mr. Garcia said, sitting down on a bench. "Grab another bat and let's see what your swing looks like today."

Luke picked up an aluminum bat from the rack, popped a token into the machine, and waited for his pitches.

It felt strange swinging another bat. It was heavier and a little harder to control than Roberto's bat. Luke found it was more difficult to direct his swing at the pitches. He couldn't adjust for the height changes as quickly as he could with the wooden bat. He swung and missed a few balls completely. When the last throw came out of the machine, Luke barely swung at it. Mad, he tossed the bat to the ground, causing it to make a loud clank on the concrete.

"Hey!" Dutch snapped from his booth. "You put that back right, Luke! I don't let nobody throw my bats, not even you."

Luke complied without a word. He grabbed the aluminum bat and quickly exited the batting cage. He stopped in front of Mr. Garcia but couldn't look at him.

"I should have used Roberto's bat," Luke said. "I hit better with it."

"It's a little of you and the bat," Mr. Garcia said. "I don't know if the bat could have helped you in there. You looked like you weren't thinking about baseball. It was like something else was on your mind."

Luke was quiet for a moment. Then he said, "My parents had a fight this morning."

"I see," Mr. Garcia said.

"They usually fight at night, when they think I'm asleep," Luke said. "They start out soft, but I can hear them. This morning was the first time I've seen them fight over breakfast. That's why I need to do better in baseball, Mr. Garcia. I need to give my parents something good to think about before it's too late."

"Now I understand," Mr. Garcia nodded, looking a little sad.

"Is there enough magic in this bat for that?" Luke asked, feeling a little angry. He picked up Roberto's bat and held it up to Mr. Garcia. "Can this bat make my parents stop fighting?"

"You got a game tonight?" Mr. Garcia asked in a calmer voice.

"Uh-huh," Luke nodded.

"Then your questions will be answered tonight," Mr. Garcia said. "Keep your arms loose and your hands relaxed, and let the bat guide you."

With that last word, Mr. Garcia simply turned and walked away. Luke felt a little bad. He felt like he had let Mr. Garcia down by the way he'd acted in the batting cage.

Perhaps Mr. Garcia was right, Luke thought. Perhaps good things will happen at the game tonight.

The first thing Luke noticed when he ran onto the field for the Sharks' game against the Auburn City Stars was that both of his parents were there to watch him play. Luke's dad smiled and waved. Luke's mom blew him a kiss, which caused Luke to look around to see if anyone on his team had noticed.

"Man, that was close," Luke sighed, snagging a throw from Thad Lockhart in center field. As was usually the pregame routine, the infielders warmed up by tossing a ball to one another while the outfielders also warmed up by throwing a ball to left, center, and right fields. After a few minutes, Luke and his teammates stopped practicing. The

Stars of Auburn City came up to bat. The game had begun.

Two innings went by, and neither team had gotten a hit. When it was Luke's turn to bat, he walked up to the plate and looked at his bat. Roberto Clemente used this bat, Luke told himself. Then he glanced up at his parents behind home plate. He wanted so badly to do something special for them. He turned to the pitcher, pulled back his bat, and took a big swing at the first pitch. He missed.

"Look them over, Luke!" Coach Futz called out from the dugout.

Luke nodded, turned back to the pitcher, and watched him wind up. The next pitch was just outside, but Luke decided to swing at the pitch anyway. He felt the bat vibrate when it hit the ball high into the air. Luke ran down to first, only to see the second baseman move under the ball and make an easy catch.

Luke's next turn at bat came in the sixth inning. By this time, his team was two runs behind the Auburn City Stars. Luke took the bat with him to the plate. He gripped the wooden handle so tightly he thought he'd crack it. In between pitches, Luke glanced back at his parents. They were smiling and clapping for him. He wanted to get a hit so badly it hurt. He wished the bat would get him just one hit.

"Strike one!" he heard the umpire say after Luke swung at a low pitch.

"Strike two!" he heard the umpire shout again after he let one pitch go right down the middle.

"Strike three!" Luke heard the umpire call out once more after swinging so hard at a pitch that his batting helmet fell off.

As he walked away from the plate, Luke turned to his parents once again. His mother had stopped clapping. His father was still smiling at him. He knew he'd have one more chance to do something special.

By the ninth inning, the Auburn City Stars had scored another run while keeping the Hart Sharks scoreless. Luke stepped up to the plate, swung at the first pitch, and hit a ground ball right to the third baseman. He sprinted as hard as he could. He ran up the first-base line faster than he thought he ever had. He jumped and tried to dive for first base only to see the ball beating him to the bag. Luke felt his arms sting when he landed in the dirt. He coughed as the dust filled his face. When he stood up, he looked to find he was bleeding from both elbows.

"Great hustle, Luke!" Coach Futz shouted, stepping out of the dugout. He turned his round body to the dugout, pointed back at Luke, and announced to the other players, "We all need to hustle like that!"

The game ended two batters later. The Hart Sharks had lost again. Coach Futz advised the players that they had another game tomorrow and that they all needed to get their rest. Luke was only half listening. He was sitting in the dugout, cradling Roberto's bat, wondering where the magic had gone. Why hadn't it worked for him?

"Honey, are you hurt?" his mom asked, meeting him on the field.

"I thought you beat that throw," his dad said, brushing the dirt off his back.

Luke didn't say much. He shrugged his shoulders, let his mom check the cuts on his arm, and then followed his parents to the car.

"Maybe you should try another bat, Luke," his dad suggested. "You might get more hits with another bat."

"Could be," Luke mumbled, dragging the bat through the grass behind him.

Later that night, a strange thing happened. Luke went right to sleep as soon as he crawled into bed. Most nights he wasn't that tired, and sometimes he would read while he listened to his parents' voices. Yet, tonight was different. Tonight something inside him seemed to draw Luke to sleep. Something was pulling him into a dream. However, even though he'd had other baseball dreams before, this one was different.

In his dream, Luke couldn't see a baseball field. There were no players running around him. Luke didn't even see a baseball or bat. Instead, Luke found himself standing on Santora Beach. The ocean was blue and gently nudged the sand. The sky above him was clear. He looked down to see he was wearing a baseball glove on his left hand.

"Hey!" he heard a voice call out.

Luke turned to see a man also standing on Santora Beach. He was taller with dark skin and a pleasant smile. He was wearing a white shirt with short black sleeves and a pair of white baseball pants. On the shirt, Luke saw the number 21 sewn in black. Luke watched as the man raised a baseball glove in one hand and a baseball in the other.

"Catch!" he called out to Luke, throwing the ball with a smooth motion.

Luke managed to snag the throw with his glove. The ball hit his glove so hard it made his hand sting a little. Luke was going to ask the man not to throw so hard when he noticed the man had slipped on a black baseball cap. Luke could see that the cap had something yellow stitched on the front of it. When he stepped closer, he saw that the yellow mark was actually a letter P sewn into the hat.

"Throw it back!" the man called out.

Luke made a low, straight throw that dropped right into the man's waiting glove. The man closed his glove, laughed, and then picked the ball out and stared at it. The way he smiled at the ball, Luke thought, was the way some men might smile at gold or some kind of long lost treasure.

"Beautiful," the man finally said. "The game of baseball is beautiful. I always loved to play. I loved it in Puerto Rico as a small boy and I loved it in America."

"Puerto Rico?" Luke said. "Is that what the P on your cap is for?"

"The P is for Pittsburgh," the man replied. "I used to play for their baseball team. Perhaps you heard of me?"

"Are you—" Luke started to say.

"Yes," the man interrupted, as if knowing what Luke was going to ask. The man stepped closer to Luke, and he recognized the face from the baseball card and the newspaper article.

"Why are you here?" Luke asked.

"Heard you're using one of my bats," Roberto said. "Well, let me tell you something. You treat that bat right, it will take care of you. Its got some . . . power to it."

"Power?" Luke asked. "You mean the kind of power to hit home runs?"

"No," Roberto answered. "I mean special powers. It'll find a way to get you hits."

"The only hits I've seen are in the batting cage," Luke said. "I tried using it in a game, but I couldn't get a hit. I tried so hard in my last game. I really wanted to get a hit because my parents were watching. Maybe your bat isn't that special."

Roberto simply smiled and nodded at Luke's words. He seemed to be carefully thinking about everything Luke had said, which not too many grown-ups did when Luke spoke to them.

"Perhaps you're trying too hard," Roberto finally said. "Sometimes I wouldn't let the bat swing. Sometimes I'd try so hard I'd mess up the magic. Maybe that's what happened when you played your game. Next time, don't try to control the bat so much. It'll lead you to many hits if you let it. That's how I got 3000 hits."

"So I shouldn't swing?" Luke asked, a little confused.

"Of course you need to swing . . . just swing with the bat. Control your heart. Keep your eyes on the ball. Don't make it so hard to do," Roberto advised.

"I . . . I don't know if I can do that," Luke said. "I mean, I want to do my best. I want us to win. If I see a pitch that I know I can hit, I just want to go for the home run. Now you're telling me not to even swing for a home run?"

Luke watched as Roberto Clemente took off his glove and walked over. Roberto held the baseball in the air and handed it to Luke.

"Why do you play?" Roberto asked.

"Huh?" Luke mumbled, trying to keep from staring at the baseball legend.

"I said, why do you play?" Roberto asked. "Do you play to hit home runs?"

"No," Luke answered very simply. "I play because I like it."

"So it's not just the home runs," Roberto observed.

"Guess not," Luke shrugged, looking down at his glove. "I just like to win."

"And what happens when you win?" Roberto asked.

"Everyone's happy," Luke answered, the faces of his parents flashing in his mind.

"You know, I helped Pittsburgh win two championships," Roberto began. He turned and stared out at the ocean. "I made my teammates happy. The people in Pittsburgh were happy. The people in my home of Puerto Rico were happy. Baseball can be a powerful thing, Luke. Sometimes it can make you think you have the power to change people. I used to believe that . . . then I found out that only the people themselves can change who they are. Not sports. Not a team. Not even a player."

"Why are you telling me this?" Luke asked.

"You know why," Roberto smiled. He looked at Luke for a moment and nodded. "Just remember the game is on the field. Don't look behind you when you're at the plate. Don't look for them. Don't play for them. Your parents will be fine. Play for the fun. If you go out for your next game and play for fun, your hits will come. I promise."

With that last word, Roberto turned and began to walk up the beach.

"Wait!" Luke called out. "I have more things to ask you! More questions!"

Roberto kept walking, heading toward a line of fog that swept in from the sea. Soon the fog swirled around Luke. The world around him grew white, before fading into darkness. Luke woke up and realized that he had just spoken with Roberto Clemente. Even though it was just a dream, he knew he'd be using the wooden bat for the next game. He knew he'd try not to look for his parents in the stands. He knew he would try to have fun. He believed what Roberto had told him. He believed he could get a hit.

8

IT'S A HIT!

The next day, Luke didn't eat much for dinner. While his parents talked to each other about polite topics like "grocery shopping" and "flowers for the garden," Luke was only half listening to them. His mind was focused on the game after dinner. Sometimes, Luke's eyes turned to his bat and glove, both of which he'd put on the counter. He thought about Mr. Garcia's story about finding the bat. He also thought about the dream and what Roberto Clemente had told him. Luke closed his eyes, made a wish for a good game, and then quickly downed a glass of milk.

After dinner, Luke and his parents drove to the field where he had a game against the Pelicans of Piedmont County. While Luke's team was able to buy matching blue hats and T-shirts for each player, the Piedmont Pelicans could afford something nicer. Piedmont was one of the richer counties in South Florida. Luke was quickly reminded of this when he saw the Pelicans take the field. They were dressed in crisp white pants with green stripes down the side, matching green-and-white shirts, and green hats with a white pelican stitched onto them.

"Look at those uniforms," Luke heard someone say.

"Fancy uniforms don't mean dirt," Coach Futz grunted. He spit a large juicy wad of sunflower seeds onto the ground. "Remember, it's not how you look but how you play that counts."

Coach Futz's words were quickly forgotten after three innings when the Pelicans put two runs on the board. The two-run lead was what Luke had to face when he stepped up to bat for the first time. He had teammates on second and third base with one out.

"Keep your eyes on the plate and the pitcher," Luke told himself as he stepped up to the plate. He forced himself not to look for his parents, Coach Futz, or any of his teammates. When he reached home plate, he simply nodded to the umpire and ignored the Pelicans catcher. He wanted to do what Roberto had suggested in the dream.

Luke planted both feet next to the plate, took a slow swing, and then pulled back his bat and waited.

His eyes were focused on the pitcher. He watched as the pitcher put both hands in the air, dipped them behind his head, kicked his leg forward, and threw a pitch.

74

Luke watched the ball come at him. Something deep within him said, "Swing." Luke could see the red laces of the ball for a split second. In that second, he could feel the bat jump off his shoulder. He didn't know how the bat jumped; it just did. Luke followed the bat's movement, swinging hard and hearing a loud CRACK fill the moment. He saw the ball fly from where he was standing and bounce perfectly between the Pelican players standing at first and second base.

"RUN, LUKE!" he heard Coach Futz shout.

Luke grinned at the bat, then dropped it in the grass and sprinted to first base.

As he ran, he saw the outfielders chase the ball to the fence. He could hear clapping and cheering from the crowd. Luke stepped on the first base bag and decided to go for more. He ran to second, easily beating the throw from the outfield.

"Safe!" the umpire called out.

Luke turned to see that both of his teammates had crossed home plate. The game was tied because of Luke. His eyes quickly turned to find his parents.

After a few seconds he found them. They were both smiling and clapping. They both looked happy. The next batter got a hit, and Luke was able to score another run. It gave the Sharks a lead they would never lose. As the game ended, Luke thought about two things—the Sharks had won their first game and his parents were happy. Luke would remember this day forever.

Throughout the rest of July, Luke did more than get one hit. In fact, he got more hits than anyone in his league. The kid who was zero for his first six games had gotten 20 hits in 24 at bats. Indeed, Luke was the hottest hitter in the South Florida Baseball League.

His hits had come in all forms. He'd gotten hits that rolled to the outfield, just past the gloves of infielders. He'd gotten hits that looped high into the air and dropped just in front of outfielders. He'd gotten hits through opponents' legs. He'd gotten hits over their heads. He'd even gotten a few hits that were so hard, a couple of players jumped out of the way. More importantly, Luke had led his team to six straight wins and second place in their division. Coach Futz even smiled twice during the six wins.

I was right, Luke thought. Winning makes everyone happy. It even made his parents happy. On the days he played, Luke went to bed at night smiling while he listened to his parents proudly talk about his play. The other days of the week, they still used sharp words and loud tones. On the days he didn't play, Luke went to bed listening to his parents talk loudly about words like "finances" and "budget." He also heard them discuss his father's job hunt, which had now extended into another month. While Roberto's words hung in his memory, Luke knew he could keep his parents together. He knew if he kept playing well, they'd forget their problems and focus on his hits and his team's wins. He could make them happy for a little while.

In a game against the Midtown Marlins, Luke got two hits off Tyrone Talbot, the league's tallest player. Luke's teammates knew that no one in the league could throw the ball faster than Tyrone Talbot. When Tyrone pitched, Luke could barely see the ball come over the plate. Yet, when Luke felt the bat jump, he quickly swung and got his hits.

Another three hits came against the Bay City Bulls. Tyler Milton was the best pitcher for the Bulls. He knew how to throw a curve ball, and he could throw it better than anyone else in the league. When Luke swung at Tyler Milton's pitches, he felt himself being pulled in different directions. It was almost like the bat was moving him close to the pitches and then getting Luke the hits.

The best pitcher in the whole South Florida League was Austin Abner of the Crestview Cranes. Luke heard some of his teammates say that Austin Abner's father used to be a professional baseball player. Austin knew how to throw more kinds of pitches than any other pitcher in the league. He could almost throw as hard as Tyrone Talbot. He could make his pitches curve like Tyler Milton. He could also make his pitches move in ways that no other pitchers in the league could do.

Yet, Luke and his bat weren't fooled by any of the pitches, getting four hits in four tries. When he got his first three hits, Luke could hear Austin's dad yelling for Austin to "use his stuff" and "strike him out." After Luke got his fourth hit, he heard nothing from Austin's dad. He had grown silent. While he stood on first base, Luke could see Austin kick the mound and smack his hand in his glove. After the game, Austin's dad went over and complained to the umpire. Somehow, he thought Luke must have been cheating to get four hits off his son. Luke knew he hadn't cheated, but it still bothered him to hear someone say it.

Instead of thinking about Austin's dad, Luke tried to focus on how his play was not only making things better for his team, but also in other places. At night, Luke heard less arguments before he went to sleep. It was as if all the old problems between his parents had disappeared.

His father's job hunt. His mother's time away from
Luke. How much she had to work. How much he
wanted to work. How little they had in the bank. All
of it seemed to be replaced by the fun his parents
were having watching Luke play week after week.

"Did you see the way Luke hit that ball?" was a
sentence he always heard his dad say the night after
a game.

"It's so exciting to watch," was usually how his
mother would answer such an observation.

To celebrate their successful month, Coach Futz
took the whole team out for ice cream after a
practice. He took the team across the street to
Mindy's Ice Cream and told them to order anything
they wanted. Coach Futz began the celebration by
asking for the Belt Buster Sundae. Luke and Thad
stood together in line and then both ordered their
favorite—a Mindy Mixer, which was a combination of
ice cream blended with three different kinds of
candy and served in a dish.

After they got their ice cream, Luke and Thad
joined some other players who were seated on a
bench. The bench faced the baseball field. The
players sat with their blue caps, eating their quickly
melting ice cream while talking baseball.

"All right, boys, got a question for you," Coach
Futz announced. "If you were lucky enough to make
it to the big leagues, what baseball record would you
like to break? It could be any record."

"Home runs!" Max Abel quickly shouted. Max played in left field. He was a short, blond-haired bundle of energy who could sprint faster than anyone on the team. "Everyone knows guys like Babe Ruth and Hank Aaron. If I broke the record for most home runs, then everyone would know my name too."

"Okay," Coach Futz nodded. "Anyone else?"

"Most strikeouts!" Mark Grace called out. "I mean, I know I play first base, but maybe one day I'll pitch."

"Very good," Coach Futz nodded. He turned to Luke and pointed at him. "What record would you like to break, Luke Tyson?"

"Number of games played," Luke quickly answered.

"You sure you don't mean most hits?" Coach Futz asked. "Or maybe number of runs batted in? How about number of batting titles?"

"No, sir," Luke answered. "It's gotta be most games played."

"Why is that such an important record to you?" Coach Futz asked.

"'Cause playing baseball is what makes me happy," Luke simply answered. He looked around, waiting to hear someone giggle, but no one made a sound.

"Okay, boys," Coach Futz smiled. "Let's eat our ice cream before it melts."

"You know what?" Thad grinned. "We've won as many games as we did all last season. Our team's playing real well thanks to you, Luke."

"It's not just me," Luke sighed.

"I mean all the hits you've been getting," Thad answered. "It's making everyone on the team play better, don't you think?"

"I guess," Luke nodded. "Feels kind of weird, though."

"What does?" Thad asked.

"Being an important person on the team," Luke said.

"Well you are," Thad said. "Just keep it up."

"These seats taken?" Mark Grace asked. Mark was the oldest player on the Sharks team. Thad and Luke looked at each other. Mark Grace never hung out with them. Luke always thought it was because they were the worst players on the team.

"You want to sit with us?" Luke asked.

"If you're not saving the seat," Mark replied.

"It's not saved," Thad grinned, clearly thrilled at having Mark Grace sit with them. "Just told Luke the team tied its win total from last season. Pretty exciting, isn't it? I mean we might make the playoffs."

"Yeah, Lockhart," Mark smirked. "I can do the math. Thanks."

Mark quickly sat down, slipped a scoop of chocolate ice cream in his mouth, and nodded at

Thad's comments. He then turned away from Thad and focused on Luke.

"Been talking to Coach Futz," Mark began. "Since you've been like . . . the best hitter on the team, me and Coach think we should move you in the lineup."

"I'm okay going to bat after Thad," Luke replied.

"You're the last guy in the lineup to bat," Mark explained. "Besides, Lockhart hasn't exactly been nailing the ball this season. A lot of times when you come up to bat, there's never anyone on base. If we put you behind some guys who get on base, we could score more runs that way. What do you think?"

Luke turned his head to Thad and noticed how his eyes were looking down at his ice cream. Luke also noticed that the smile was gone from his face.

"Guess that would be okay," Luke said.

"Good," Mark said, "I'll tell Coach. Now if Lockhart could start getting a few hits, maybe we could move you back."

"I'll try," Thad mumbled.

"Before the season's over would be nice, Lockhart," Mark said, standing up and leaving.

"Sometimes Mark can be a real jerk," Luke said.

"He's right, though," Thad admitted. "I haven't been getting any hits."

"You're just in a slump," Luke said. "You'll snap out of it."

"Luke!" Coach Futz called out. "Come here! I want to go over the new batting order with you and Mark."

"Guess I better go," Luke said.

"Guess you better," Thad mumbled.

Luke stood up and started to walk to his coach. He turned for a second to see Thad sitting alone, eating his ice cream and staring at his feet.

9
SOMETHING TO PROVE

Usually around the halfway point in the season, the South Florida Baseball League held a picnic for all its players and their families. This year, the picnic was going to be at a baseball field in Hart County. When Luke arrived with his parents, he saw blankets of every color spread around the green grass of the outfield. He heard music playing from a band that was set up near third base. Behind home plate, Luke saw a line of grills that were sending streams of smoke into the bright blue sky. When some of the smoke reached Luke, he could smell the grilling hamburgers and hot dogs.

"Over there's a spot," he heard his mom say.

Together, Luke and his father followed his mom through a narrow lane of grass that separated families on their blankets. As he walked, Luke recognized some of the faces of kids who were eating with their parents. Luke guessed that the ones he didn't know were from teams he hadn't played yet.

"This looks like a good spot," Luke's mom said, stopping in her tracks. She reached under her arm and pulled out a maroon blanket. She held the blanket in the air, letting the wind open it, and then lowered it to the ground. She dropped on the blanket and began to unpack a small picnic basket of drinks, plates, napkins, and chips.

"So, what are you hungry for?" Luke's dad asked.

"Hot dog sounds good," Luke replied.

"I think I'll have a hot dog too," Luke's mom said. Her eyes gazed into the picnic basket, and she didn't really look at Luke's dad. "Maybe you could get them for us?"

"Guess so," Luke's dad answered without looking at her.

Luke watched him quietly walk over to join some other fathers who were gathered around the grills. Luke watched one father hand his dad a drink, while another father slapped him on the back and laughed about something. Luke turned to see his mom finish unpacking the picnic basket.

"I think I'm gonna walk around a little," Luke said. "See if I can find anyone from my team."

"Don't be too long," Luke's mom warned. "Food will get cold."

While he wandered around the baseball field, Luke heard a familiar voice.

"Hey, Luke."

Luke turned to see Thad standing behind him.

"Hi, Thad," Luke said, managing a smile.

"They're doing some kind of throwing contest over there," Thad said, pointing to center field. "Feel like checking it out?"

"Sure," Luke replied.

As they walked, Luke could see a group of kids standing in a long line. They were all waiting for something. At the front of the line, Luke could see a man handing a baseball to the first person in line. Luke could also see a backstop a few yards away. The backstop had a round target set up behind the plate. Another man stood alongside the backstop holding some type of plastic gun. Luke watched him aim the gun at each throw.

"Wonder what that guy's got in his hand," Thad said, pointing at the plastic gun.

"It's called a radar gun," a voice answered from behind them.

Luke and Thad turned to see Austin Abner standing behind them. Not only was Austin the best pitcher in the South Florida League, he acted like it.

Austin smirked at Thad.

"What's it used for?" Thad asked.

"For speed, stupid," Austin laughed.

"They're using the gun to see how fast players can throw a baseball," Luke explained.

"Right, Luke," Austin said. "Last year my older brother threw the fastest pitch here. My dad said he throws so hard that some major-league team might sign him up after high school. He's standing over there on the pitcher's mound watching them throw. C'mon over . . . I'll introduce you to him. His name is Kyle."

Luke stood still while Thad followed Austin over to where his taller, older brother was waiting. Kyle was a good foot taller than Thad, with blond hair that poked out from under a red baseball cap. Kyle's eyes were narrow and his smile was barely visible when Luke watched him shake Thad's hand. Thad quickly waved Luke over to where he was standing with Austin and his brother.

"Luke," Austin grinned, "this is my brother, Kyle."

"Hi," Luke smiled.

"So you're Luke Tyson," Kyle replied, barely cracking a smile. He looked Luke up and down. "My brother says you're the best hitter in his league. Heard my dad talk about you too. Don't look like much to me."

"Kyle has the fastest pitch in the state," Austin bragged.

"Almost as fast as a major-league pitcher," Kyle explained. "My dad says I got a few years to grow till that happens."

"Wanna see what it's like to hit against one of the fastest pitchers in the state?" Austin asked.

"Don't look at me," Thad said, throwing his hands in the air. "I like baseball, but I don't want to get killed."

"How 'bout you, Luke?" Austin asked.

"I don't think so," Luke replied. "Besides I don't have a bat."

"Brought one along," Kyle said, reaching to the ground next to the mound. He pulled up an aluminum bat and held it out to Luke.

"No, thanks," Luke answered, sensing a trick.

"You know, Luke," Austin began, "my father is talking about having you investigated for using an illegal bat."

"What?" Luke answered, feeling his face grow hot.

"He's talked to some parents, and they think you're hitting so well because of that old wooden bat," Austin explained.

"That's a joke!" Luke snapped, getting angrier at each word he heard.

"My dad's a lawyer," Austin said. "He knows a lot about rules and laws. I think he knows what he's doing unless—"

"Unless what?" Luke asked.

"If you could use this bat to get a hit off my

brother," Austin said, "maybe I could tell my dad. Maybe I could let him know how you got a hit off Kyle without your bat. Might just change his mind about reporting you."

Luke stood silent for a moment. He was furious that Austin's dad was going to try to take his bat away. Luke thought for a moment. He knew he couldn't let them take the bat. With that one thought, Luke turned to Kyle and grabbed the aluminum bat from his hands.

"Go ahead and throw me your best pitch," Luke said, walking back to home plate.

When he reached the plate, Luke turned and glared at Kyle standing on the pitcher's mound. Luke gripped the bat tightly, the anger pouring through his arms and hands. He watched Kyle's dark eyes stare down at him. Luke noticed that one side of Kyle's mouth curled up, like a little smile. Without hesitation, Kyle kicked up his leg, leaned back, and threw a pitch.

Luke watched as the ball seemed to cut through the air at a speed faster than anything he'd seen in the batting cage. Luke's eyes followed the ball as it curved in and began to head right for him.

Luke closed his eyes, turned his head, and tried to step back. Somewhere in his stomach he felt a round burning feeling push against him, driving the air out from his body. Luke dropped to the ground, barely aware of the bat falling from his hands.

"Luke!" he heard Thad shout. "Are you okay?"

Luke was flat on his back. He stared up at the blue sky, struggling to take a breath of fresh air. Suddenly a flood of faces surrounded Luke's view of the sky. Voices began talking loudly while Luke tried to breathe. He wanted to say something, but nothing was coming out of his mouth. Luke was scared.

"I'm a doctor," he heard a man's voice say. "Leave him there. Don't move him!"

Luke felt hands feeling his chest. He felt an ear brush against his mouth—he assumed it was to see if he was breathing.

"I'm okay," Luke managed to say.

The doctor sat him up and felt around his rib area, lifting up his T-shirt to examine where the ball had hit. "Just got the wind knocked out of him," he announced as he continued to examine Luke. "His ribs feel good. No unusual bruising. He should be fine."

Luke stood up with some help. Then he looked across the crowd around him and saw Kyle and Austin standing together. Kyle simply stared at Luke without any expression on his face. Then he turned and walked away. Austin walked over to Luke with a grin on his face.

"Trying to get yourself killed, Luke," Austin laughed.

"It's gonna take more than your dad or your brother to stop me from playing," Luke snapped, poking Austin in the chest with his hand.

"Hey, Luke, it was an accident," Austin said, the smile vanishing.

"Your brother won't stop me and neither will your dad," Luke spoke loudly. "Next time you play me, I'm gonna nail every pitch you throw. That's a promise!"

Right after that sentence, Luke's parents descended on him. His mother lifted his shirt and checked his stomach for any bruises or marks. His father asked Luke what had happened and then went off to find Austin's father.

"Your son did that on purpose!" Luke heard his father shout.

"Your boy was crowding the plate!" Austin's dad yelled back.

Luke simply turned and began to walk away. His stomach felt like something was pressing against it. In the distance, he could still hear his dad arguing with Austin's dad.

"You okay?" Thad asked, appearing out of nowhere.

"Yeah," Luke answered.

"Can you believe him?" Thad asked, bouncing next to Luke. "He can't strike you out, so he gets his dad to take your bat and his brother to hit you with a pitch."

"No one's taking my bat away," Luke said, his heart pounding at the thought.

Together, Luke and Thad walked around the grounds for the rest of the evening.

Every so often, Luke would pull up his shirt, rub his stomach, and look at a small bruise.

As they were walking, Luke could tell that Thad wanted to say something.

"So how did you get so good?" Thad finally asked.

"Huh?" Luke mumbled, still lost in his anger for Austin.

"I've kinda been wondering," Thad said softly, "how you got to be so good."

"You saying that because of Austin?" Luke asked.

"No," Thad answered. "I've been thinking about it for a while. I mean, you and me were always about the same when it came to baseball, you know? We had the same number of hits last year and we were about the same this year . . . until now."

"You're right," Luke nodded. "We always were about even."

"When I'd strike out in a game," Thad recalled, "I knew it was okay because you'd strike out at least once. When I wouldn't get a hit, I'd know you wouldn't get one either. I knew I wasn't the best player on the team . . . but it was okay because there was always someone that was just like me on the team. Now . . ."

"Now there isn't," Luke said.

"Like I said," Thad began, "I was just wondering how you got to be so good. The way I figure it, maybe I could get good too. Then I wouldn't be the only bad player on our team."

"Well," Luke said, thinking about how to answer the question. "Every morning I stop by the batting cage at Santora Beach. There's a guy I see there sometimes who gives me some help on my swing. His name is Mr. Garcia. He used to be a baseball scout."

"I remember you talking about him," Thad said.

"He was the old man who gave me that newspaper," Luke said.

"The one about Roberto Clemente," Thad remembered.

"Right," Luke said.

"Think he'd give me some pointers?" Thad asked.

"I'm sure he wouldn't mind," Luke answered. "Come on around the batting cage some morning. It'll be fun. Besides, if you get to be good, then our team would really be hard to beat."

Luke stood quietly listening to Thad go on about his swing and how much he'd like to beat Austin's team. No matter what happened, Luke knew his next big game wouldn't be on the baseball field. He knew that Austin's dad would talk to the league commissioner and try to take his bat.

The next morning Luke decided to do something he hadn't done for a while. He decided to walk down to Santora Beach after his paper route. He decided to go back to the batting cages and, if he was lucky, talk to Mr. Garcia about everything that had been happening.

93

It was a busy day at Santora Beach. Since it was the peak of summer, there were more people coming in from the city to visit. The sun was hot. The beach was bright and the sand kicked up with the wind. The ocean looked blue and cool to Luke as he walked down the path next to the beach. When he got close to the batting cages, Luke could see Mr. Garcia seated on a bench next to Dutch Howard's booth. Luke walked faster. There was so much he wanted to tell Mr. Garcia.

"A face from the past," Mr. Garcia said, smiling at Luke. "How are you, Luke Tyson?"

"Fine," Luke said, parking his wagon next to the bench. He sat down on the bench next to Mr. Garcia.

"Haven't seen you for a few mornings," Mr. Garcia observed.

"Guess I've been getting enough batting practice with my team," Luke answered, pulling out some coins from his pocket. "Been getting a lot of hits during my games."

"So you're doing good?" Mr. Garcia asked, pointing to the bat in Luke's wagon. "Bat still being kind to you?"

"Yes, sir," Luke answered with some pride in his voice. "I'm the best hitter in the league right now . . . and I'm not even sure how I'm doing it."

"That's the good thing about having a special bat," Mr. Garcia stated. "Don't need to think too much. Just let the bat do the work. That's the secret."

"I know," Luke sighed, his eyes turning to the ground, the smile vanishing from his face.

"What's the matter?" Mr. Garcia asked.

"Mr. Garcia," Luke began. He stopped for a moment, folded his arms, and took a deep breath.

"What is it, Luke?"

"You think I'm cheating by using Roberto's bat?"

"Goodness no," Mr. Garcia replied. "Why would you think that?"

"There's this pitcher I know," Luke explained. "He plays for another team. His dad thinks that my bat must be rigged because I've been getting a lot of hits with it. I guess he's gonna talk to our league's commissioner about me and the bat."

"It's just a wooden bat, Luke," Mr. Garcia grinned. "Let them have the bat. They can see for themselves if they want. Don't worry about it. The bat is perfectly legal."

"I know," Luke said. "Just makes me mad. I mean, my parents are so happy right now because of the way I'm playing . . . I just don't want it to end. I don't want my parents to go back to the way things were."

"And how were they?" Mr. Garcia asked.

"Sometimes . . . they'd fight about money," Luke mumbled. He paused for a moment and could still hear their loud voices in his head. "It's not like they always would fight. They didn't used to be like that. It's just that . . . since my dad lost his job, we're kinda poor I guess."

"I see," Mr. Garcia sighed.

"Can I ask you something?" Luke began.

"Of course, Luke," Mr. Garcia replied.

"Dutch Howard said you used to find good baseball players to send to the big leagues. He said you were some kind of a scout. Is that true?"

"Yes," Mr. Garcia nodded.

"I was wondering," Luke began, his voice growing softer, "do you know of a team that I could play for someday? That would make my parents really proud and happy. You know how well I can hit with this bat. I mean, I hit in the fastest batting cage. Maybe I'd be good enough to play for a pro team. What do you think?"

Mr. Garcia quietly listened to Luke's words. When Luke finished, Mr. Garcia thought about the question, his eyes fixed on the ground. He thought longer than most grown-ups did when Luke asked a question. Luke watched Mr. Garcia rub the white whiskers on his chin, then look at Luke and smile.

"What do you think . . . honestly?" Luke asked again.

"Honestly?" Mr. Garcia replied. "I know you can hit. With that bat, I'm sure you can hit better than most grown-ups who come here. There are other things you'll need to do as a pro baseball player, Luke. Big-league teams want you to run faster than most grown-ups. You'll also have to throw harder, farther, and with more accuracy than a lot of grown-ups.

Then you'll have to be on the road a lot and away from your family for months. What do you think?"

"I guess I'll have to just wait and see," Luke sighed.

"Let me tell you a story," Mr. Garcia began. "There was one year when Roberto Clemente played his best. He felt really good about it, and when the votes were taken for the league's best player, you know what happened?"

"He won?" Luke guessed.

"No," Mr. Garcia replied. "In fact, he didn't even come in second or third. Not only did he finish behind other players, he even finished behind one of his teammates. Roberto was happy for his teammate, but deep inside he was crushed. It was one of the most disappointing moments he ever had as a baseball player . . . or so I was told by those who knew him well."

"So what did he do?" Luke asked.

"He tried harder," Mr. Garcia explained. "Every year he went out and had a season that was even better than the last. He proved to everyone he was the best baseball player on the planet. Finally, Roberto was voted MVP for being the best player in baseball."

"Why are you telling me this?" Luke asked.

"Here's the reason," Mr. Garcia explained. "Someone as great as Roberto Clemente found himself in a situation where he could have easily given up. Nothing was the way he wanted it to be, but he kept trying. He kept trying, and he found a way to make things better. I don't know what's happening with your parents, but sometimes things have a way of working out. They did for Roberto. Maybe they will for you."

Luke took another deep breath. It made him feel good knowing that someone like Roberto Clemente knew what it was like to be sad or disappointed. Those were two things grown-ups didn't talk about very much, and sometimes Luke felt as if he were the only person in the world who felt a little sad about how things were with his family.

"So what should I do?" Luke asked.

"Worry about things that other kids your age are worrying about," Mr. Garcia suggested. "Worry about your team winning. Worry about getting a hit. Worry about doing your best because it's something you want, not because you think it will keep your parents together. Baseball is supposed to be fun. I think it's about time you have some fun playing it."

Luke nodded to Mr. Garcia. Then he stood and walked over to Dutch Howard. He put his coins on the counter and waited for Dutch to give him a token.

"Hope you hit a home run," Dutch grinned.

"Thanks," Luke answered.

He walked over to the batting cage, picked up his bat from his wagon, and then selected a batting helmet. He turned to see Mr. Garcia taking a seat on a bench, ready to watch Luke get some hits. Luke took a deep breath, put his token into the machine, then stood next to the plate and waited. Was it the bat or was it him? The question lingered in his mind. Then he had an idea. It was a strange idea, but it would be a good test to find out the reason for his incredible play.

When the first pitch came out, Luke saw it for a split second then closed his eyes. Without thinking, he took a swing at where he thought the pitch was going to be. Suddenly, he felt a vibration start at his hands and work its way up both arms. He heard a loud crack. Luke quickly opened his eyes and laughed when he saw the ball fly away from him and into the netting behind the ball machine.

"Oh, my gosh," Luke mumbled to himself. He turned and grinned at Mr. Garcia for a split second.

For the next four pitches, Luke did the same thing. He saw the ball appear from the machine. He closed his eyes. He imagined where he thought the ball should be. He swung and heard the familiar crack of ball on wood. Five times the machine pitched balls to him. Five times he closed his eyes and swung. Five times he got hits.

For the last five pitches, Luke kept his eyes open. He watched each ball leave the machine and shoot across the plate. He watched each ball so closely he could have sworn he saw the red laces on the balls.

He also used his bat to nail five straight hits, all of which shot around the pitching machine in the batting cage. When the machine turned off, Luke stood next to the plate for a moment, bat on his shoulder, his hands gripping the handle, and his eyes turned down.

"I guess it's a tie!" Luke shouted. "Five hits for the bat and five for me. I guess you were right, Mr. Garcia! Maybe I should have more fun!"

He turned and looked back at the bench. There he saw that Mr. Garcia had vanished during Luke's ten hits. Luke looked up and down Santora beach. There was no sign of Mr. Garcia anywhere.

CHALLENGES

When he returned to his house, Luke saw a strange car parked in the driveway. It was dark blue and looked kind of familiar. As he drew closer to the door, he heard his father talking to someone in the kitchen. Luke opened the door to find Coach Futz seated at the kitchen table with his father. When the door slammed shut behind Luke, both men stopped talking, turned, and smiled.

"Morning, Luke," Coach Futz grunted from his chair.

"Hi, Son," his father smiled. "How was your route this morning?"

"Okay," Luke said, stepping into the door. "Morning, Coach Futz. How come you're here?"

The question hung in the air. Luke stepped up to where both men were seated and saw a piece of paper on the table. It was a small paper that had Luke's name written on it along with the day, month, and year he was born.

"Luke," Coach Futz began, "I don't know how to put this. Never had this happen in the years I've been coaching Little League here in Hart County.

Now I know you've been working real hard this season and that your hard work has finally started paying off with all these hits you've been getting. You've gone from the basement to the top in batting average not just on the team, but also in the league. Got a few parents who've noticed that and . . . well, they just want to be sure that it's all on the up and up."

"I don't understand," Luke said.

"Some folks think you're too old to be in the league," Luke's dad explained. "Coach Futz came here today to ask me for a copy of your birth certificate. We both know you're the right age to be playing; it's just that some parents want proof. Coach Futz will take care of that problem."

"I bet Austin Abner's dad was one of them," Luke mumbled.

"Now, Luke," Coach Futz explained. "I'm not gonna sit here and give you a list of names to get worked up about. It was more than one parent, but we'll take care of them. Count on it."

"Austin said his dad was all but calling me a cheater," Luke recalled. "I know his dad's gotta be part of this."

"It's none of the players, Luke," Coach Futz said. "It's just a couple of parents."

"So is that it?" Luke asked. "They just want a piece of paper?"

"A copy of your birth certificate . . . and one more thing," Coach Futz answered.

"What?" Luke's dad spoke up. "I mean, my gosh, what else could these people possibly want?"

"Luke's bat," Coach Futz answered softly. "Seems that some of the parents have taken a notice to the bat because it's one of the few wooden bats in the league. They also noticed how Luke started . . ."

"Started what!" Luke's dad pressed.

"They uh . . ." Coach Futz began, then paused. "They think the bat might be rigged with something. They think Luke's been getting more hits with it, so they want to look at it. Make sure there's no funny business with it."

"I don't like this," Luke's dad said, slamming his fist on the table. "My son goes out and plays an honest game the best he knows how, and this is what people do? This is how people congratulate him for improving so much? This is a joke!"

"You're right," Coach Futz replied. "These are rich people who don't like to see their kids fail. And when someone makes them fail, like Luke causing them to lose, then parents get upset and decide to do something about it. If we give them the bat and the certificate, they won't have anything more to cry about. What do you say, Mr. Tyson?"

"The bat doesn't belong to me," Luke's dad replied. "I'm afraid that it's gonna be Luke's decision."

"How about it, Luke?" Coach Futz asked.

"I don't know," Luke mumbled. "What do you think I should do, Coach?"

"I can't answer that," Coach Futz smiled. "I can give you my best guess about what could happen. The league's commissioner is friends with one of the parents who's complaining. I'd guess if you gave up the bat and the certificate, all this would be over with pretty fast and you'd keep playing. If you decided not to give up the bat, then . . ."

"Then what?" Luke asked.

"My guess is this group of parents might think you're hiding something. They might try to get you off the team," Coach Futz said.

"What!" Luke's dad shouted.

"They might say Luke's not following the rules," Coach Futz explained. He turned to Luke. "Now of course, I can't tell you what to do, but our team needs you. We're better with you than without you, Luke. I hope that helps you make a decision."

Luke quietly stood up and went outside. He could hear his father's angry voice charge at Coach Futz. Luke walked over to his wagon, pulled out the bat, and held it in his hands for a moment. He gripped it tightly with his hands, turned it a couple of times, and watched the sun shimmer off the wood.

"I think I could do it," Luke told himself. "I think I could be just as good without the bat. I'd like to try."

He turned and walked into the house. Coach Futz and Luke's dad stopped talking when they saw Luke appear with the bat. Luke held it at his waist, gripping it tightly with both hands. He sat down at the table and slid the bat over to Coach Futz.

"It belongs to a man named Sonny Garcia," Luke explained. "He owns a sports store down by the beach."

"Yeah," Coach Futz mumbled, "I know Sonny real good. Used to be a professional player for a time till he wrecked his knee. Was a pretty good scout for a couple of years too. Brought up a lot of talent from Puerto Rico."

"When you told us about going to the beach, you didn't mention Mr. Garcia. Who is he?" his dad asked.

"He's been helping me with my swing at the batting cages," Luke confessed. He turned to his dad, whose face looked a little red. "I know you and mom tell me not to talk to strangers, but he seemed nice. I checked him out with Dutch Howard who runs the batting cage. He knew Mr. Garcia too. Anyway, Coach Futz, Mr. Garcia's the one who gave me the bat. If you have any questions, you should call him about it."

"I'll pass that along," Coach Futz said, standing up. "I'm proud of you, Luke. Not a lot of boys would be doing this. I'll tell them to put a rush on the decision."

"Thank you," Luke answered.

Coach Futz held out his hand, grabbed Luke's hand, and shook it. Coach Futz then stood and nodded to Luke's dad. He took the birth certificate and the bat with him and then slipped out the back door.

"Man," Luke's dad sighed. He rubbed his face with both hands, stood up, and wrapped his arms around Luke. "Being good at something shouldn't be like this, Son. It shouldn't be a punishment or a claim of dishonesty. I just want you to know how proud your mother and I are of you. How proud we've been at the way you've improved as a baseball player. But more than your baseball play, I'm most proud of you for what you did just now."

"I know," Luke answered, holding on tight to his father and not wanting to let go.

Later that afternoon, Luke lay in the grass with his ball and glove. Luke lay in the narrow yard, looking up at the violet clouds that moved above him. He tossed his ball into the air and caught it with his glove.

He could hear the sound of his mother's feet stepping through the grass toward him. He turned his eyes to see her standing right beside him. He could feel her hand reach out and touch his hair as she sat down. He sat up.

"Your dad told me everything," Luke's mom smiled. "He said you did the right thing. Said you made him proud. If you made your dad proud, then I'm proud too."

"Good," Luke nodded.

"So why are you sitting here looking so sad?" she asked.

"I'm not sad," Luke answered, "just worried."

"Worried about what?" she asked.

"About how I'll play next game," Luke answered, tossing his ball in the air and catching it. "I mean, what happens if I don't have my bat for our next game? What if I go out there and strike out every time I step up to the plate? I'll let my team down and I'll let you and Dad down."

"I don't know about your team," Luke's mom smiled, "but I don't think you could ever let your father or me down."

"Since I've been playing better," Luke observed, tossing the ball in the air again, "you and Dad haven't been fighting as much."

"Fighting?" Luke's mom said, her voice rising. "What do you mean, Luke?"

"Sometimes at night," Luke began, holding the ball in his hand, "sometimes right before I go to sleep, I can hear you and Dad argue about stuff. I mean, it's not that I try to listen. It's that my bed is right next to your wall and sometimes—"

"You can hear us talking," his mom interrupted.

"Some nights I can hear you argue about when the phone bill is due, or when the electric bill is due, or when dad will get a job, or how much you don't like your job," Luke recalled. He tossed the ball into the air and caught it. "Ever since I started playing better, I don't hear you and dad fight . . . I mean talk like that at night. When you go to bed, you both talk about my baseball games and you sound . . . different. You both use normal voices. You don't yell.

It's just . . . nice. I don't want things to go back to the way they were, the way they were before I started playing well."

"Oh, honey," Luke's mom sighed.

"Hey, Luke!" his dad called out, sprinting from the house. "Just got off the phone with Coach Futz. We have an appointment this evening to meet with the South Florida commissioner at the library. Coach Futz said the commissioner wants to talk to you about your bat. I bet if things go well, we can have the bat for your next game."

Luke and his parents arrived at the new Hart County Public Library around 7:00 in the evening. Luke had seen the outside of the building a few times when they drove by, but he was always too busy to go inside. Luke remembered hearing his parents talk about how the library got the local jail to help with the move. How some prisoners helped to move all the books into the new library when it was finished. When he heard this, Luke thought about every book he'd taken out of the old library and wondered what type of criminal had carried it into the new library.

Luke followed his parents up the steps and then paused to look at the tall white columns that marked the library's entrance. Once inside, Luke and his parents moved across the dark green rug that ran under towering bookshelves and into every corner of the library's main room. They moved between the large wooden shelves that stretched up to the ceiling.

"Isn't this beautiful?" Luke heard his mother whisper.

His dad stopped in front of an older woman who was carefully taking books off a cart and sliding them onto a shelf.

"Excuse me," Luke heard his dad say. "Is there some sort of a meeting room around here?"

"Straight back," the older woman replied, waving her hand in the direction they were moving. "Can't miss it."

Together, Luke and his parents walked past the shelves, beyond a set of tables and chairs, and then around a corner where they found an open door.

"This must be it," Luke heard his dad say.

When they stepped into the doorway, they found a giant stained glass window bursting with color from the setting sun. Beneath the window three men and two women sat talking at a long wooden table. Suddenly a tall, slender man stood and walked over to them. He held out his hand, smiled, and came right up to Luke.

"You must be Luke Tyson," the man grinned, grabbing his hand and shaking it. "Thank you so much for coming here today. My name is Hayden Grant. I'm the commissioner for the South Florida Baseball League. I've been following your numbers this last month. You've had a heck of a season, young man."

"Thank you," Luke said, a little embarrassed at the comments and the attention.

"And these must be your parents," Mr. Grant said, reaching to shake their hands.

"Nice to meet you," Luke's mom said with a slight smile.

"Hello," Luke's dad said with not so much as a grin.

"Please, sit down," Mr. Grant said, pointing to three chairs across the table from where the others were sitting. Luke sat down across from an older man with thick round glasses and a dark suit. Luke smiled at the man, but the man did not smile back. It made Luke feel a little uncomfortable, so he turned his eyes to Mr. Grant who didn't seem to have any difficulty smiling.

"Aside from myself," Mr. Grant began, "we also have the South Florida League Baseball Board of Advisors here today."

"Who are they?" Luke's dad asked.

"Parents of former players. Folks who love baseball and don't mind helping out from time to time. I asked them here to get their thoughts on what Luke will say here today," Mr. Grant explained.

"You okay?" Luke's mom whispered.

"Yeah," Luke said, his eyes glancing at each face at the table.

"Mr. Secretary, you may begin," Mr. Grant said.

"We are here today to determine whether

Luke Tyson should be allowed to continue to play for the Hart County Sharks."

"Allowed?" Luke's father said, sitting up closer to the table.

"Your son has repeatedly broken a league rule, Mr. Tyson," a woman with bright red hair spoke up.

"What rule would that be?" Luke's mother asked.

"Rule 7 of the South Florida Little League manual clearly outlines a weight limit for baseball bats to be used by its players. Your son has been using a bat that is too heavy and therefore does not meet the rules as set forth by the league."

If anything, Luke thought, the bat felt too light to him when he swung it. Luke turned to see Mr. Grant reach down and pull up the bat. He carefully placed it on the table and slid it down to Luke. The sight of the bat brought a smile to Luke's face, and he reached out and touched it with his hand.

"It is a beautiful bat," Mr. Grant sighed. "Don't see too many players in the South Florida League who like to use wooden bats. Where did you get it?"

"From a sports shop," Luke answered.

"Doesn't look that new," Mr. Grant replied.

"It's from a shop down by Santora Beach," Luke stated. "Sonny Garcia is the name of the man who owns the shop. He's the one who gave me the bat. He said I could use it for the summer."

"I know Sonny Garcia," Mr. Grant nodded. "I thought he owned a sports shop with antique sports stuff in it, a shop with sports items that are very old or have great value to them."

"He does," Luke answered.

"So this is more than just a baseball bat," Mr. Grant pressed.

"Mr. Garcia said it once belonged to Roberto Clemente," Luke said.

The room grew silent. Luke could feel every eye at the table focus on him. He looked down at his hands and tapped them on the table.

"The Roberto Clemente?" the man with the big glasses asked Luke.

"Yes, sir," Luke replied.

"I think you're lying," the man with the big glasses mumbled.

"Our son doesn't lie!" Luke's dad snapped.

"How dare you," Luke's mom hissed.

"There's no need for such a comment," Mr. Grant said, casting an angry look to the big-glasses man. "I believe Luke is being honest."

"Of course he is," Luke's mom said.

"As I said," Mr. Grant began, "I know Sonny Garcia. If he said that this was a bat that belonged to Roberto Clemente, then it's probably true. Now, Luke, I am curious as to why Mr. Garcia would give you a bat that once belonged to such a famous person."

"He thought it would help me with my swing," Luke answered, choosing not to reveal too many details about the bat. "Every morning I walk down to the beach and use the batting cages there to practice my swing. Mr. Garcia saw me there a few times. We talked. Then one day he gave me this bat to use. I've been getting hits ever since."

"Even though you were breaking a rule," one woman spoke up.

"I didn't know there was a rule about weighing bats," Luke answered.

"You are supposed to know all the rules in the South Florida League," the man with the big glasses explained. "It was in your registration packet we mailed to everyone who wants to play. Didn't you read your forms?"

"Excuse me," Luke's dad spoke up. "My son is the best person I know. Baseball is the best game I know. When my wife and I go to see my son play and cheer him on, it's the best feeling in the world to us. Now I don't know about rules for bat weights. I don't know about any registration forms. I do know I'm not going to sit here and listen to a group of adults argue with my son over things that are . . . ridiculous!"

"These rules are not ridiculous," the woman with the bright red hair said.

"Our son made a mistake," Luke's mom spoke up. "What rule do you have for forgiving a boy who makes a mistake?"

Luke sat back and watched his parents. He watched them both begin to speak loudly, but not at each other. He noticed how they sat close to the table and sometimes pointed at the people on the other side. Luke couldn't help but smile. What he was seeing was better than he'd imagined. These were his parents, fighting for him, working together to defend him. Somehow, he knew he didn't have to be the best anymore.

"Luke," Mr. Grant finally said. The other voices in the room grew silent when he spoke. "When I deal with players who break rules in this league, I ask myself two questions: did the player intentionally break this rule, and will the player do it again. I get a sense that you honestly didn't know about the rule regarding bat weight. I don't think you broke this rule on purpose. I guess my next question would be in regards to the bat. If I gave it back to you, would you continue to use it?"

Luke grew silent to think about the question. He looked down, and out of the corner of his eye he saw something incredible. There he spotted his mother's hand holding his father's hand, their fingers neatly laced together. His dad's thumb gently rubbed the back of his mom's hand.

"I don't need it anymore," Luke announced. He looked at the bat, ran his hand over the wood grain one last time, and then slid it across the table back to Mr. Grant. "If you know Mr. Garcia, you can give this to him. Tell him I said thanks."

"Are you sure?" Luke's dad asked. "We can fight this, Son."

"It's okay, Dad," Luke replied.

It was the last thing Luke said at the meeting. He sat quietly staring at the bat on the table while the grown-ups spoke. Then, without warning, Mr. Grant reached out, grabbed the bat, and removed it from the table. Luke watched him pull it to the floor.

A few minutes later, when the meeting was over, Luke watched as Mr. Grant walked around with the bat tucked under his arm. Luke noticed how he smiled.

Some of the grown-ups patted Luke on the shoulder. A few told him what a "mature" boy he was for making such a decision. One man leaned down to Luke and told him he had made the right choice. While he listened to their comments, Luke watched Mr. Grant leave with the bat under his arm. He noticed Mr. Grant and another parent studying it in the parking lot. As Luke got into his car with his parents, he wondered if the men could feel the magic too.

THE MAGIC

The next morning, Luke returned to the batting
cage after his paper route. He paid Dutch Howard,
walked over to the cage, and slipped on a batting
helmet. He grabbed one of the aluminum bats from
the rack and held it for a moment. Luke thought it felt
kind of strange not having the wooden bat anymore,
but he knew it was important to try using an
aluminum bat before his next game. As he headed
over to the cage, he spotted Mr. Garcia walking from
his shop.

"Morning, Luke," Mr. Garcia said with a wave.

"Morning," Luke replied. "Thought I'd try to get used to swinging a new bat."

"Yes," Mr. Garcia nodded as he approached Luke. "I heard about your decision."

"So how do you think I'll do?" Luke asked.

"As well as you did in your last game," Mr. Garcia replied without hesitation.

"But I won't be using Roberto's bat," Luke pointed out. "I won't be that good."

"Remember what I said to you before I gave you the bat?" Mr. Garcia asked.

"I'm not sure," Luke replied.

"I told you that the bat came with a story," Mr. Garcia explained. "Now I don't know how true the story is . . . but part of me likes to believe it."

"So you don't know if it was really Roberto's bat?" Luke asked.

"Not for a fact," Mr. Garcia replied. "I wasn't on the beach. I didn't see it wash up on the shore. I'm just taking someone else's word for it."

"So how will you know for sure?" Luke asked. "I mean, could you call this person and ask him again?"

"I don't think I'll have to do that," Mr. Garcia said. "I think that bat gave you something. Call it confidence. Call it the ability to believe in yourself. I don't need to make a phone call to know if the bat has magic in it. I know what I've seen. I know what I believe."

"But how will you find out for sure?" Luke asked.

"When's your next game?" Mr. Garcia said.

"Tonight," Luke answered.

"Then I guess we'll find out tonight," Mr. Garcia replied. "Remember, keep your arms loose. Your grip relaxed. Your eye on the ball . . . and we'll see what happens."

"That's easy to say," Luke sighed.

"Come here," Mr. Garcia said, with a wave of his hand. Luke followed Mr. Garcia over to the beach. Mr. Garcia stood silent, staring out at the ocean. "You know they have a story about this beach. They tell me that there's a hidden treasure around here. A hidden treasure that's just waiting to be found. Now most folks go looking on the beach for that treasure. This summer I think I may have found that hidden treasure. I think I may have found that treasure every morning, in the batting cage, taking swings."

"Me?" Luke said, a little surprised.

"When I watch how you play," Mr. Garcia began, "I see a lot of good things. Now I've seen plenty of baseball players in my life, but none of them had as nice a swing as you do. I want you to go out there tonight and show everyone what you've shown me all these mornings. Show them what I've seen. Show them what happens when you swing a bat."

Luke recalled Mr. Garcia's words for the rest of the day. He remembered them while he cut the grass. He remembered them while he ate his dinner. He remembered them in the car while his parents drove him to his game against the Crestview Cranes.

"Look who's here! Luke Tyson and his toothless Sharks!" Austin Abner yelled from the Cranes dugout. "They don't look so tough today."

Luke watched as Austin sprinted across the field to where Luke and his teammates were standing. Austin got close to Luke and grinned.

"Bet you're not so tough without your bat," Austin said.

"I might not have my bat," Luke replied, "but I keep my promises. You remember what I promised you."

"You're gonna go down swinging, Luke Tyson," Austin stated with a big, broad smile across his face.

In the first inning, Luke's team was unable to get a hit. Austin Abner was throwing harder than he did the last time he had pitched against them. Perhaps, Luke thought, he was psyched up to strike out Luke and the rest of his team. Austin's dad glared at Luke whenever he ran off the field. Luke knew that Austin's dad was waiting to see if he could still get a hit without Roberto's bat.

"Luke, you're up!" Luke heard Coach Futz announce in the second inning.

Luke walked over to the Sharks' equipment bag. He dug around with both hands until he found a bright silver aluminum bat. Luke pulled the bat from the bag, tapped it on the ground, and then walked to the plate for the first time in the game.

"Look over your pitches, Luke!" Coach Futz called out—the same old advice.

"Here we go, Roberto," Luke said to himself.

He kept his eyes down as he walked to the plate. He tried to concentrate on what he was about to do. He gripped the aluminum bat with all of his strength. When he reached the plate, Luke took a deep breath. He relaxed his arms and his grip on the bat.

On the mound, Austin Abner stared down at Luke. Austin's bright red hair poked out from under his dark baseball cap. His mouth hung open. His eyes seemed to stare right through Luke.

Trying to stay calm, Luke took another deep breath. He pulled back his bat, lowered his shoulder, and stared at the hand in which Austin was holding the ball. Luke watched Austin wind up. He watched Austin step forward on the mound. He watched the ball appear from Austin's hand and get launched into the air. Something deep in his heart told Luke this would be the pitch. This would be the pitch that Luke could swing on with all his heart.

PING!

Luke watched the ball fly high and deep. He began to run to first base while he watched the outfielder run backward for what seemed like minutes. When the outfielder bumped into the fence, Luke heard his team cheer loudly. He saw the outfielder throw down his hat. He saw the ball drop into the grass just beyond the outfield fence.

"That's a home run!" the first base umpire said to Luke. "Keep running till you touch home plate!"

"I—I know," Luke said, standing on the first base bag for a few seconds. It was the first home run anyone on his team had hit all season. It was also the first home run Luke had ever hit in a game.

As he began to run to second base, then to third base, and then home, Luke thought about what had just happened. He saw his parents smiling and clapping for him. He felt the pats on his back from his teammates. He saw Austin Abner kick the dirt on the mound. Even Coach Futz was smiling. With one swing, Luke had brought happiness to the people he cared about the most. Best of all, he'd done it with a regular bat.

In his second at bat, Luke smacked a pitch just past third base and into the outfield. Luke got to second on this hit, then looked to see Austin Abner frowning at him. Luke simply smiled and stood on second base.

A little later in the game, Luke brought two of his teammates home to score with a solid hit to center field that flew over the outfielder's head. This hit put the Sharks ahead for the first time in the game, causing Luke's teammates to chant his name for the first time all season.

"This is so cool," Luke said to himself as he stood on base.

After the hit, Luke saw the Cranes coach walk out to the pitcher's mound. It looked to Luke that the coach wanted to put in another pitcher for Austin Abner, but Austin refused to leave the mound. Austin's dad jogged out from the stands and, after talking to the coach, was able to keep Austin in the game.

In his final at bat, Luke hit the ball just over the head of the Cranes player at second base. As he ran, Luke watched the ball drop in for his fourth hit of the game.

Austin Abner yelled something to the person playing second base. Then Austin smacked his glove with his fist. Luke simply stayed on base and watched Austin Abner have a temper tantrum on the pitcher's mound. Luke tried not to smile too much while he listened to Austin tell all of his teammates how badly they were playing.

Luke was certain that Austin's bad temper helped the Sharks to an easy victory over the Crestview Cranes. It was a game that Luke knew he had helped to win without Roberto's bat.

The next day Luke went straight home after his paper route. He walked into his bedroom and grabbed two pieces of paper off his desk. He had spent an hour the night before writing on them, trying to find the right words. Then he went to the garage and searched through the recycling bin for a glass bottle. He shoved the papers and bottle into his backpack and rode away.

When he arrived at the beach, Luke was surprised at what he saw in the batting cage. There he found Thad standing in the cage, swinging wildly at every pitch. Luke stood silent for a few seconds but didn't see Thad get a hit. Still, he was out there trying to get better, and Luke felt good knowing he had given Thad the suggestion.

Luke parked his bike in front of Mr. Garcia's store. He hopped off the bike, ran up the steps, and opened the door. When he stepped inside, he found Mr. Garcia leaning on the counter reading a newspaper. He looked up, smiled at Luke, and then turned his eyes back to the counter.

"There's a story here about a baseball player for New York who hit four home runs last night!" Mr. Garcia said. "Imagine that, four home runs in one game? Just when you think you know the game, you read something like this and it knocks your socks off. Guy steps up to the plate four times and hits four home runs . . . ain't that something!"

"That's a pretty amazing story," Luke said.

"So what brings the star of the Hart Sharks to my store?" Mr. Garcia asked, folding up his newspaper.

"I was wondering if they gave you back your bat," Luke said.

"Yes, they did," Mr. Garcia said, looking up from his paper. He pointed to a glass showcase beside where he was standing. Luke went over, his eyes focusing on a long brown bat displayed on the top shelf of the showcase.

"Good," Luke smiled. "I was worried that they wouldn't return it."

"Me too," Mr. Garcia sighed. "I do believe that bat has still got a lot of magic left in it. You showed me that, Luke. You saw what it did for you, for your team. I could only imagine what it would do for a major-league baseball player. If word got out, some big-league player would be offering me millions of dollars for it. I mean, what player wouldn't want to set a new record for home runs or for batting average? This is the bat that would do it. Yes, I'm glad it's been returned. It belongs in this showcase where its magic is safe. So what did you learn from all this?"

"Learn?" Luke asked.

"About being the best," Mr. Garcia smiled. "Is it what you imagined it would be?"

Luke thought for a moment. In his mind, all he could see were his parents smiling at each other.

"Being the best . . . it's okay," Luke nodded, "as long as you have people to be happy with you."

"What do you mean?" Mr. Garcia asked.

"You know," Luke began. "In that newspaper you gave me, I read about how much Roberto Clemente loved his family. How much he loved his mom and dad, his wife, his children. I kind of think he needed them around to feel like he was the best. I think he needed them to share it with or it wouldn't have meant as much to him. Do you think that's true?"

"Maybe," Mr. Garcia smiled.

"I brought something for you," Luke said, reaching into his pocket. He pulled out a folded piece of paper and passed it to Mr. Garcia. "My mom always says you should thank someone when they do something nice for you. She's really into writing thank-you notes and stuff like that. I didn't have a card or anything fancy like my mom sends, but I wanted to thank you."

"What for?" Mr. Garcia grinned.

"For giving me some batting tips," Luke began. "For lending me Roberto's bat. For trusting me to use it. The first time you asked me why I wanted to be the best, it was because I wanted my parents to stay together. Now . . . my dad just found out he got a job and things are back to the way they used to be. My parents don't fight anymore, and I think it's because of that magic you were talking about. The magic from Roberto's bat."

"That's very nice of you, Luke," Mr. Garcia said. He paused and pointed out the window to the batting cages. "Now I couldn't help but notice your friend is trying to practice his hitting in one of the cages this morning. What's his name again?"

"Thad Lockhart," Luke replied.

"Yes," Mr. Garcia nodded. He winced while he watched Thad almost fall down after one big swing. "Well, I do believe I should give poor Thad some pointers before he hurts himself."

"You gonna loan him a bat?" Luke asked.

"I don't think so," Mr. Garcia said, walking around the counter. "Just a few helpful tips should be enough for young Thad. Why don't you come along and help."

"I can't," Luke said. "Got something else to do first."

Mr. Garcia noticed that Luke was holding a clear bottle in one hand. He watched Luke pull out another piece of paper, roll it up, slide it into the bottle, and then put a cork that he had taken from one of his parents' bottles in it.

"Remember when you told me about how Roberto's plane crashed in the ocean?" Luke asked.

"I remember," Mr. Garcia said.

"And you said that they never found Roberto?" Luke asked.

"That's right," Mr. Garcia nodded.

"So it's like he just disappeared somewhere out there," Luke said.

"I guess so," Mr. Garcia replied.

"Just wanted to be sure," Luke said, pushing the cork farther into the bottle. "Thanks."

Luke left the store, hopped on his bike, and rode down the walkway a little. When he found a part of the beach without anyone around, he parked his bike, took the bottle out of his backpack, and began to walk out through the bright white sand.

The wind blew. The sand was hot. Two seagulls, wings stretched out, glided along a breeze that led them out to sea. The waves curled in from the water, turning chalky white before crashing on the sand. Luke watched them for a few seconds, listening to the sizzling sounds each wave made before rolling back into the sea. Then, without warning, the ocean grew calm. The wind swept away. Luke found himself surrounded by a moment of silence and stillness.

"This is for you, Roberto," Luke quietly spoke.

He reached back and as hard as he could, threw the bottle high and into the water. He watched as the bottle bobbed on top of one wave before sliding down its back and drifting out to sea. Luke stayed for a while, watching the sunlight flicker off the bottle as it was slowly carried away. He walked along the shore, straining to see the bottle above the high

waves that started to come in. He squinted at the
bottle when the wind began to blow sand in his eyes.
He stopped walking when the bottle, and the note
inside it, had vanished into the ocean. He hoped
somehow, somewhere, it would find Roberto.

Dear Roberto,

Thank you for letting me
use your bat.

Thank you for leaving some
magic in it. I think the magic
helped me and my team get
better. I think it also helped
my parents stay together.
The bat taught me that I can
do something if I relax, close
my eyes, and have confidence
in the magic in myself.

Luke